Salt House

Salt House

A NOVEL

Hazel Hawthorne

Afterword by Allison Bass-Riccio

PROVINCETOWN ARTS PRESS

Published by Provincetown Arts Press
P.O. Box 1677, Provincetown, MA 02657
provincetownarts.org

First Provincetown Arts Press edition, 2025

Originally published in 1934 by Frederick A. Stokes Co., New York, *Salt House* is reprinted here by arrangement with the Hazel Hawthorne Archive, courtesy of Allison Bass-Riccio.

Cover and book design: Irene Lipton

Cover photographs: (front) Jeffrey Love, *Seaward*, 2024; (back) Walker Evans, [Hazel Hawthorne Werner], 1929–34, ©The Metropolitan Museum of Art, image source: ArtResource, NY

Cartography: Jake Coolidge

ISBN: 978-0-944854-39-6

Printed in the United States by Puritan Press, Inc.

To M. R. W.

I learned this, at least, by my experiment: that if one advances confidently in the direction of his dreams, and endeavors to live the life which he has imagined, he will meet with a success unexpected in common hours.

— *Henry David Thoreau*

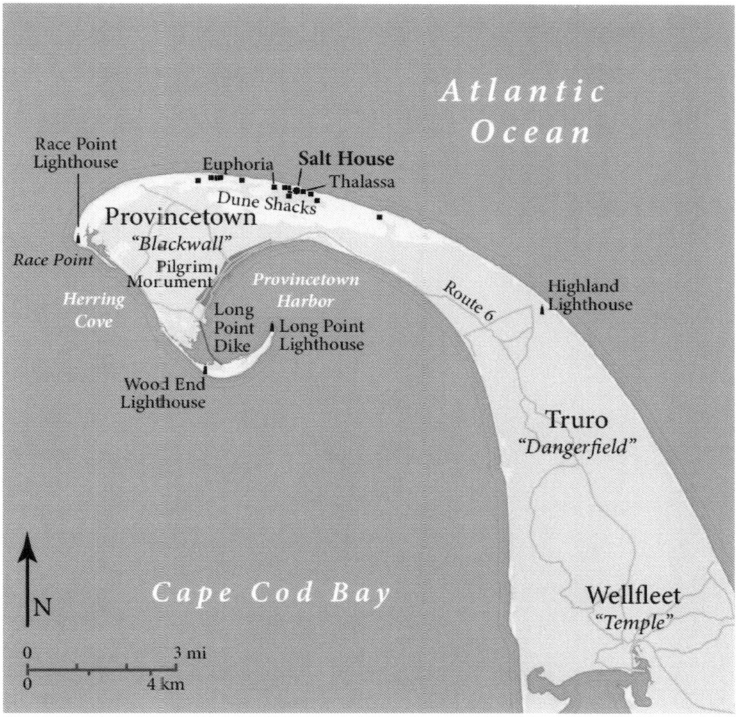

Outer Cape Cod

The outermost towns of Cape Cod — Provincetown, Truro, and Wellfleet — are shown here with the names given them by Hazel Hawthorne in this novel. The location of Salt House, where much of the story takes place, is marked where the Peaked Hill Bars Station stood. This life-saving station, owned by Eugene O'Neill after it was decommissioned, was known to Hawthorne and inspired her fictional creation. The dune shacks Euphoria and Thalassa, acquired by her in the years after *Salt House* (1934) was published, are also shown. They continue in use today.

Preface

Hazel Hawthorne's novel *Salt House* has long had a legendary status in Provincetown — the small town at the tip of Cape Cod where Hawthorne spent many summers living on the dunes on the "back shore," and later in a cottage in town. Published in 1934, the book is known by locals, who treasure their rare copies, as presenting an authentic picture of the bohemian life of the town and the dune dwellers, as told by someone with first-hand knowledge.

The novel gives us much more, though, than a depiction of Provincetown, the storied art colony and refuge of rebels and outsiders. Written in the form of a journal, it traces the inner life of a woman — the book's protagonist, Judith — who breaks away from social conventions, determined to find her own path on her own terms. Scholar of 1930s literature Paula Rabinowitz calls it "a lost feminist gem." As such, it fills in a missing link in US literature, standing as a foremother to the Beat literature that, after World War II, would pick up with the themes Hawthorne explores in the interwar period: bohemian life, free love, critical perspectives on America, the Road. Like painter Alice Neel (1900–1984), whose work has recently attracted new interest, Hawthorne shows us a side of America in the late 1920s and early '30s that we need to know more about, populated by artists, pacifists, socialists, queer people, and other nonconformists.

In bringing *Salt House* back into print, Provincetown Arts Press aims to make the novel available again to readers everywhere, and, through the book, offer access to the singular setting of the Province Lands and the surprisingly modern story of an iconoclastic woman.

HAZEL HAWTHORNE

Hazel Hawthorne (1901–2000) was born in Maine. The death of her father when she was about twelve pushed her toward early independence. She worked at various jobs, including modeling, and visited Provincetown while a teen, possibly drawn by the presence of her cousin, Charles Hawthorne, who had established an art school there. Later she recalled her first encounter with the dunes while babysitting the children of writer and activist Mary Heaton Vorse, a Provincetown year-rounder.

Hawthorne would return to Provincetown in 1920 with her first husband and, for the first time, stay in a dune shack. The couple was based in Massachusetts, where he was a Unitarian minister and taught at Harvard. Hawthorne began writing during these years, primarily poetry, while also having five children.

Following a bruising divorce in 1929, which was covered in the national press, Hawthorne came to Provincetown on her own, initially with her children, though custody was contested. The events of *Salt House* probably reflect some of her experiences during this period. A few years later she remarried, to Morris Werner, an editor and writer, residing with him in Greenwich Village but always summering on the dunes, and eventually moving to Provincetown full-time around 1981, after Werner's passing.

As her writing developed, Hawthorne published short stories in the *New Yorker* and other venues and a second novel, *Three Women* (1938). Her occasional writings appeared in magazines including

Provincetown Arts (published by Provincetown Arts Press).

On the Cape, Hawthorne became an advocate for the preservation of the dunes and dune shack community. For more on this, the two dune shacks Hawthorne eventually owned, and a deeper look at Hawthorne, see the afterword in this volume by Allison Bass-Riccio.

THE SETTING OF THE NOVEL

Although *Salt House* fictionizes Provincetown as "Blackwall," the novel's setting is unmistakable as the outer tip of Cape Cod, where the Province Lands have remained a wild landscape of dunes and low forest, edged by the Atlantic Ocean. As early as the 1850s, structures were built near the water to house life-saving operations: The Peaked Hill sandbars, just off the shore, were the site of numerous shipwrecks. Small shacks served as outposts, too, for life savers and others who desired to stay overnight near the water.

In 1919 the Peaked Hill Bars Station, by then decommissioned, came to be owned by playwright Eugene O'Neill, then a key member of the Provincetown Players, the group that had produced his first play, *Bound East for Cardiff*, in 1916. Hawthorne stayed in and near the station several summers, beginning in 1920, and it provides the basis for the Salt House of her novel — the house on the dunes where Judith and other characters stay. In her fiction, Hawthorne transforms O'Neill's life-saving station into a salt works, a type of operation that made salt from sea water. Salt works dotted Cape Cod in the nineteenth century but were on the way out in the twentieth. Hawthorne would have known that there had been salt works on Long Point, across the harbor from Provincetown, and at other locations near the town.

As life-saving became less urgent because of modern navigation methods, the dune shacks on Provincetown's back shore became dwellings for locals and artists who appreciated the landscape and solitude. Today the dunes are part of the Cape Cod National Seashore, and the shacks are maintained by local families, who have passed them down over generations, as well as by the Peaked Hill Trust and Provincetown Community Compact. These include the two shacks that Hawthorne owned, Euphoria and Thalassa.

The map of Outer Cape Cod on page ix shows locations named in *Salt House* as well as today's landmarks.

THE TIME OF THE NOVEL

Salt House is composed of the journal entries of the main character, Judith, spanning June to October of one year, but the year itself is not given. The novel thus has an aura of timelessness. However, clues to the general time period include references to World War I, which is clearly in the past, and to Prohibition, which is clearly ongoing (it would end in 1933). In addition, the characters mention a book that was published in 1930, and at one point quote from a play produced on Broadway in 1930 (for details, see the notes in the novel's text). Given these markers, the time of the novel can be identified as circa 1930.

PREPARATION OF THE TEXT

The text of *Salt House* reproduced in these pages follows the original edition with minimal changes. Some adjustments have been made to modernize punctuation, and in one place spelling is changed to avoid racial caricature. While some of the book's vocabulary, especially relating to race, is outdated, we have kept it unchanged as it reflects the language considered most respectful at the time when the book was written.

Livia Tenzer
Book Committee
Provincetown Arts Press

For additional information online, see:

"Finding Hazel Hawthorne," Inka Leisma (creator). Podcast, 10 episodes. 2020.

"Peaked Hill Bars Station Site," U.S. Life-Saving Service Heritage Association. https://uslife-savingservice.org/station-sites/peaked-hill-bars.

"Provincetown Dune Shacks, Remarkable and Never Repeated," New England Historical Society. https://newenglandhistoricalsociety.com/dune-shacks.

Acknowledgments

Provincetown Arts Press wishes to thank all those who made this new edition of *Salt House* possible: first and foremost, Allison Bass-Riccio, steward of the Hazel Hawthorne Archive, who generously and enthusiastically supported the project from the beginning, giving us access to documents and photographs in her collection and helping research key aspects of the novel, in addition to writing an afterword for the book that offers her personal reflections on *Salt House* and Hawthorne's larger legacy.

With her students at the Cheshire Academy, Bass-Riccio prepared the transcription of the novel used to produce this book. We offer heartfelt thanks for this labor of love to the following Hazel Hawthorne Archive Project interns: Ava Provite, Emma DiBenedetto, Allison Fowler, Maria Togonidze, Layna Paul, and Maya Kerr-Harris.

The press extends a special thanks to Susan Pomerantz, granddaughter of Hazel Hawthorne, for providing information about Hawthorne's life and for spurring us forward to complete this project. We also owe thanks to the Provincetown Public Library: The library's copies of Hazel Hawthorne's books, as well as papers relating to her life in its Provincetown History Preservation Project collection, were critical to the production of this volume.

At the press, the idea of bringing *Salt House* back into print was proposed by book committee chair Livia Tenzer. We thank her for her dedication, support, and work, which made this book possible. We also thank the members of the committee, John DaSilva and

Irene Lipton, the press's creative director, who designed this volume; and Ingrid Aue and Sally Rose, who consulted on many questions along the way. Thank you, also, to Michael Broder of Indolent Books and Anne Hegeman of Duke University Press, who offered helpful advice on production and printing.

Generous support for Provincetown Arts is provided by the Massachusetts Cultural Council, the Provincetown Cultural Council, the Sylvester Family Foundation, the Ritchie-Davis Foundation, and many individual donors and readers, without which we would not have been able to undertake this project.

Most importantly, Provincetown Arts wishes to thank all those who maintain the dune shacks that have been so important to the cultural life of Provincetown: the Peaked Hill Trust, the Provincetown Community Compact, and the families who preserve individual shacks. We believe that Hazel Hawthorne would be delighted not only to see *Salt House* return to print but also to witness the community of people on the dunes continuing to flourish.

Elizabeth Winston
Executive Director and Editor
Provincetown Arts Press

Part One

June 1 — When I approach the town of Blackwall from upshore and see its mist-drenched outlines across the harbor, I long to possess it again — at once! I really have the most presumptuous feeling that I own the place. It is a bold town, curving a bay, backed with austere hills of sand, wind, and the loud strong Atlantic.

I came here this morning, and with a few clothes and books in a gunnysack over my shoulder, crossed the dunes by the Salt House Hitch. The day was bright and cool, rich with the whole season to come. A wall of sand rises where the footpath leaves the woods, and soon beyond begins a line of planks laid end to end. Those planks lead over the Hitch until they reach the banks overhanging the back shore. When I topped the rise, halfway out, I saw the flat blue sea again, the first time this year. My eyes visited the tower and every window and porch of the coastguard station, then traveled across the irregular horizon to the north, where Feargus's shack stands like a child's alphabet block left on a slope of grass, and then, still north, to the shapely dune beyond which stands Salt House.

What surprised me as I stood on this threshold was that I was empty as the valley. Here was the actual place, in panorama, where I am to undertake a new life, quite different from what I have known before, and by the very intensity of recognition it seemed unreal, or like a dream, that is, bound in some of its parts to be imperfect. At any moment I would be meeting Philip Hatefield, whom I had not seen in eight months, whose name I had repeated day and night for two years — yet I was passive.

Everyone who comes here admits this blunting surprise, which proceeds from having been cut off so suddenly from the smaller landscape satisfactions he has obtained elsewhere, and from which he is aroused only after many days on these slumbrous dunes and on this always resounding shore.

Nothing moved except slow masses of cumulus clouds overhead; there was not even a ship on the water. I went down the long slope and over the pale thighs and breasts of the dunes toward the house.

Salt House is the only building left standing of all those once attached to salt works along the coast.[1] Hence it has a historic interest and is frequently surrounded by tourists, but they are disappointed in it, for there is no longer a windmill, and the intricate system of reservoirs, falls, and vats has crumbled into dingy sand. Because of its unmannerly isolation few people want it, and I find it easy to rent, season by season. It lies in the lee of a dune, so low that one may walk up the roof and enter by the tower, with gray shingles laid over it like flakes of ash.

It is late now, as I write. I am lying in a pile of blankets in the room under the tower. Philip isn't here.

As soon as the sun went down, the chill of early spring returned, and after supper Feargus and I huddled in the kitchen in rocking chairs. I was glad to see Feargus. When I came near the house he was standing in the doorway, and "Judith!" he cried, with his arms wide. I rubbed his chest with my fist. "You sun-worshiper, you! Now you must be jaunty and tell many stories and many lies, with a woman in the house once more."

I find that he ensconced himself here last winter, quite in the way of a burrowing animal, and I don't mind saying, despite my devotion, that he has put the three rooms in which he lived into an evil disorder. One of his letters, however, puts another light upon it, shows the way *he* saw it: *Brought ram-cat heater from maid's room and rigged to flue with nondescript pipe from barn. Set up large bed with two mattresses, head toward the sea. A ham-tree in the pantry and a rainbow round my shoulder. Can put up any flaming beauty you send this way, one at a time.* He says that sometimes the silence offended his nerves so that he went into the storage room and shouted and roared. I can imagine it, in that cold dim room, like a mad hermit, unless he's just tonight devised the picture to amuse us both.

Properly speaking, he has no right to be living in Salt House, but I told him to move over the hill only at his own convenience, that he is welcome here and we shall always want him near us.

We? Philip and I.

The panes in the kitchen windows have all been scratched by blowing sand, since they weren't shuttered during the winter. It was good to be in that room again, with its filmy light. The three square windows, side by side, are above the table, facing a high bank outside, so that as we eat we look up at grass that waves against the sky like whole pampas plains in miniature.

Almost I saw Philip in the corner by the lamp shelf, as he was the first night of our acquaintance. He had come stumbling in out of the darkness with packages Feargus had left on the Hitch for him. I offered whiskey, so that he wouldn't go right away again. When he sat down, the lamplight touched up his dry yellow hair springing back from between his bare temples. He had the high brows and large features of a movie actress's face, except for the nose too thin and nostrils flared wide open.

But I don't quite like that resemblance. If it is true, it is also a little sinister. I don't know — there's something — why doesn't he come?

Perhaps he will arrive in the middle of the night, either by the door or by the tower.

The ladder to the tower stands beside my bed.

That night he turned his eyes from one side of the kitchen to the other in embarrassment, and I marveled at his irrelevant way of speaking. I remember that I felt flushed and gay, and that was as much the effect of his shining yellow hair and white perfect teeth as of the whiskey. I leaned forward in my chair, pressing my hands tight between my knees. I am not often sure of myself, but that night I was brimming with confidence. I was wearing my blue overalls, old ones with the straps torn off and the frayed edges pulled up under a broad leather belt, and also a blue jersey and a red handkerchief tied under my chin. Those swaggering clothes smelled of the stable. Just then I was a woman who could sit a glittering horse (never mind that Jezebel is only a mustang, if that!), drink whisky neat, and take any man she wanted.

Feargus became slower of speech as he drank, with a total effect of sacerdotal dignity. Once he rose to stir in the depths of a crock of wine and recited the recipe to us. "Yeast boys at this stage," he said, "are amoebic and can easily be shocked out of their socks. Virgins following this recipe should never be négligé."

I felt that he didn't really like Philip. That is why, tonight, I mentioned him at first only as to a stranger. "He is coming back here; he's working his way from the West." And then, to my own surprise, I asked, "He *is* a fine and sensitive person, isn't he?"

Feargus thrust out his legs, folded his big soft hands over his belly, jutted his under lip, in short, looked as rotten as ripe with wisdom.

"Sensitive to the point of weakness," he said. Then I saw Philip as from his letters: in the desert facing purple hills, on a rock pile over the border, sketching whores in Mexican saloons, driving his truck across the horizons, all the time wild and lonely as a dog . . .

When I started up the companionway stairs Feargus loaded my arms with blankets.

"Rake sleeps up there sometimes," he said, "but he's a tough youngster. You'll need more covers."

"Rake?"

"A boy — my friend. Rakiot Basque, the artist's son — a philosopher in his way," he chuckled. "You'll see him one of these days."

For six good feet the army blanket up here was indented.

Every time the wind stirs I think it is a footstep upon the roof. The surf is very loud, the night is cold and vaporous.

June 2 — I worked all the morning getting the shutters off the rest of the windows. It revives an old dizziness in Feargus, he tells me, to climb a ladder, so I wrenched off the upstairs ones by myself.

Philip, by the way, has not appeared.

It was a hot day, with the sea flat as a plate. It was very difficult getting the shutters off the sea chamber; finally I had to smash a pane from the inside. My face and hands were burned, my whole body seemed to be expanding from working in the sun. Sometimes Feargus came over the hill from his shack to see how I was getting on.

"I am calling it The House of the Interpreter, out of *Pilgrim's Progress,* you know," he said with a backward wave of his hand.[2]

"I wish you and Philip to think of it that way." His face was almost stern with his whimsy.

Standing on the ladder I heard the roar of the turbines of a passing freighter, and also the intermittent toneless notes of the bell buoy. I've settled my things in the sea chamber. It has not been touched since last year, and yet there is no dust, only a sprinkle of sand that rippled in through the winter. There are lockers under one slope of wall and a wide wooden bunk under the other. The white-painted walls take the changes of weather as does the underwater. This room is less protected from the sea than the rest of the house, and no matter how low the surf, its tumultuous vague sound is sure to be heard. No one is going to take the sea chamber away from me.

June 3 — He didn't come yesterday, or last night.

I have prepared the whole house, all but the rooms that Feargus inhabits. These, the pantry, kitchen, and the boiling room, where once the bitter water was stored until the cold weather, when crystals of Epsom salt formed after its boiling — these rooms are so dirty that I have to assume fortitude in moving about them.[3] This vivid, static dirtiness also breeds the spirits of abandonment — but suddenly I rushed to the sea chamber and sit there now at the desk, my head in my hands, legs twisted around the chair, in rebellion against the hairs, dead ashes, burnt matches, and grease. They are my dead body, for I have become alive to the rest of the house — I touch it and it is as much a part of me as my own body. I should think Feargus would have whispered that, too, in the midst of his passionately solitary winter.

June 4 — Nothing is as important as his coming. For hours today I have been lying on the dune above Dead Men's Hollow. The clouds have a faint copper tinge along their upper billows. The glass porch and windows of the coastguard station return the light as touches of quartz gleam in pebbles on a distant shore. The water is as pale, as blue, as a pale blue silk ribbon.

There are spears of new beach grass growing like a fence around me, yet I can see across the valley to the top of the path. No figure looms there except those scheduled to appear from the coastgaurd station: the man on liberty and the man who gets the mail, who climbs the Hitch at quarter of twelve and descends it again at quarter of four. These I know, and they are my indications of time, for the blue wooden clock above the fireplace has not yet been set in motion. I need no time other than the accurate hour when he will arrive. I lie here watching, and like a pregnant woman whose hour is nearly upon her I am neither afraid nor angry — by now I have even gone beyond eagerness.

Later — Feargus called from the doorway, "Here's a bit of beauty," and when I went out, there was the moon sharp as new tin.

June 5 — Yesterday, after writing in this journal, I dragged myself up off the sand, which after all is ages deep and firm, so that transient bones begin to ache, and I went into the house and found Feargus puttering about over a fish. I forgot to record that I went out on the north patrol two nights ago, returning in a fair wind with Joe, one of the coastguards. Suddenly he rushed down upon a whiting that moved in the wash of the surf, and when we got back to the house he gave it to me. Feargus took charge. He is never slothful when it comes to food, and whatever is gathered up from the dunes or shore stirs his imagination to the point of an actual talent.

As for Joe, I opened a bottle of beer for him, and we drank it with solemn thirst. Feargus went to his bed in the boiling room. We had only a candle for light, the blue flame of the oil stove for the heat, and there was something of conspiracy in this midnight drinking. The brass handle of Joe's Coston light and the nickel of his flashlight caught the flame in bracelets. We talked about the past winter, of the loneliness here, and the way the sea has torn in under the banks and hollowed out a bay, and of the shifting bars. "No good is coming to this place," Joe said. "The way the wind drives the tide in from the northeast, Salt House is sure going to be washed out to sea."

After he had put on his raincoat and watch cap again, and with his light pointed a path out by the north door, I turned down the flame and went to bed. Why don't I go on patrol more often? You don't talk but press your body into the wind until your haunches ache; the salty air dries your throat, and then afterward the beer tastes cold and sharp, and gives you deep sleep.

This day is dark and moist; the sky is blue with wind.

I would have been riding Jezebel on such a day, but she is still being boarded by a bootlegger friend in the next village.[4]

All the morning I crouched by the cave of the fireplace in the storage room. I should have gone to town for food, as there is very little left, but I have so much to think about that I shall delay as long as possible.

I know why I am here. What we must do is feel; the limit of

nonfeeling is death. And as, for me, there was no feeling elsewhere . . .

The storage room seems buried, as perhaps actually it will be some day. Already sand falls down the chimney and crackles in under the windows, for outside it is rising year by year along the wall. The casements are high, so the room is like a deep white cellar, and I always have a feeling that any life that has been here is retained and goes on echoing and being known.

A portfolio of Philip's pictures has come, and I dared to lift one out, the first my hand touched upon. It was one of his early flesh-confused abstractions. It lies on the floor: I lean over it and see that the figures resemble him in some way, that they simplify his personal real beauty. I am moved and I whisper, "You fair, you gentle!" And then I think, "Whatever is reaching and growing in me is met in you. We should do well together."

It was here, in this room and on such a day, though later in season — indeed, on the very day when autumn fell — that he came the second time. It was afternoon; the fishing boats were standing in close to shore, the sky was dark, with a strange livid light flowing out from under the clouds.

"I am expecting a friend for tea," I said to the maid, and crouched before the fireplace laying sticks.[5] Then I paced through the shadows of the room thinking ferociously, "It has to begin — I am ready for it to begin, and here, today!"

June 6 — Bright hot morning. A clean and energetic sea neatly defines its edges with incessantly forming scallops of foam.

He has not come. I don't even know where he is. I have stopped listening for him, for his coming seems something I imagined earnestly. I thought he would not knock or call but enter the door and come straight to wherever in the house I would be, and I kept thinking there would be no unnecessary words, but the quiet of Salt House, the long stretch of its summer days like a tunnel — dark and moist, with light at either entrance.

My longing has overreached itself, and I am tired of waiting. I am going to swim, then put on a silk dress — nothing else, so that I'll feel clean as nudity — and go to Blackwall. If Feargus is anywhere about he may want to go, too. No doubt we'll stop by the hollow tree beyond the railroad tracks where Feargus keeps a bottle of gin to restore his flagging energy going and coming along the Hitch.

A brilliant mist has descended.

Returning — and I will not forget this — we followed footprints over the sand. We both felt the importance of these prints in our lives. There was no question of their being those of a stranger, for they were definitely toward the house, made steadily in that direction. "Can it be?" I asked, but after some conjuring Feargus admitted that it was probably only Rake. I was excited; the prelude was over — someone had stepped into my waiting. As we rounded the last of the dunes and went down the cutting to the house, Feargus said, "Even if it's only Rake, I wish you to be very kind to him."

For no reason we always shout as we near the sunken porch which stands against the house like a box. I was trembling as I listened for the answering voice. It came, a young man's voice, but it was not

Philip, and it troubled me as a thing which I could not stop, short of turning back and going away.

We pushed the door and stepped down over the threshold, and felt like going into a hole in the ground. I blindly held out my hand to take the hand of a boy who thrust black hair out of his eyes, answering, "Yes, this is Rake. And you are Judith?"

The footprnts had led to him; it was too late now.

June 7 — It is morning of a fair day, with delicate clouds, no wind, and a long slow surf. Feargus is below in the kitchen; Rake sleeps upon the blue divan in the storage room. Philip is not here, and I shall not repeat this again in my journal.

Rake has a camp in the woods off to the west, between the dunes and the town. He has been coming out here occasionally, to talk with Feargus and to make beer, and that is why he came last night. He is nineteen years old, and high-flavored. His hands are playful yet indecisive, like puppy paws; he has freckles, gray eyes and rank black hair, and his eyebrows are inked low and brush across his nose. Feargus says he sleeps sixteen hours out of the day, for he hasn't expanded in proportion to his height, and it's true that he has long narrow bones with the flesh but meagerly pulled over them, and a flat boy's chest, plainly arched and high. He allows feeling to add luster to what he sees, but for the most part, I think he is unformed. Of the two worlds in which he moves — himself and circumstance — only the latter, outer world is continuously tangible, perhaps because he is always quietly, pleasantly drunk.

Last night we ate together, fresh fish begged from the incoming boats, tomatoes in salt and oil, and Portuguese bread. I saw that Rake wore dingy clothes and ragged sneakers. I wanted to attract him and ran upstairs for a touch of the perfume I have been saving for Philip. I was shocked as I did this and, as before the mirror, I studiously decided to tie a narrow silk ribbon around my hair.

After supper we walked, all three, up the shore toward the sunset. A span of clouds fled around the sky with outstretched necks and greedy mouths. At the final bloody western explosion their purple, gold, and flamingo-pink feathers went drifting down into a motionless dark bank along the wide horizon. Then the evening chilled and we turned back, climbing the dune on the northwest side of the house. Feargus, in his best paternal way, suggested that Rake remain with the lady and tell her stories while he went in and brewed some coffee. Rake shyly demurred, then submitted. He sprawled on the sand, chewing a pull of grass, and we both looked toward the water suffused for those few moments with a warm rose color. We could not dissolve easily into each other; so far we are only soluble in Feargus.

At the base of the day we went inside to drink the coffee and smoke. Night came hesitantly, as if from afar. Feargus drank much beer and became fitfully tedious. We questioned — he stated that the negro's god is white.[6] And then, when we had done with this, he told of the Spanish influenza epidemic in Alaska, of fourteen dying Eskimos in a mission building in Nome who hanged themselves in a single noose, one at a time, helping one another until the last one swung alone with no one to cut him down. And of the Catholic priest who gathered up bodies for burial in the springtime, frozen men and women piled head to heel, and dragged them through the streets on a sled.

Feargus tries to accomplish in talking what he hasn't done in writing, and the seasoned elaboration of the good material of these stories was almost more than my restlessness could bear.

I went into the storage room and made a driftwood fire. Rake followed, and we lay flat on the hearth until the night was half gone. An old bucket, from off the shore, became a flower when its glowing hoops slid down and it fell apart. The petals, being saturated with dry salt and covered with pitch, lay burning in purple and green and white, as well as in the clear yellow and red of ordinary fire. Once Rake put his hand on my hair and rubbed my skull, with teasing fingers. A cricket sang from some unknown niche behind a panel. We talked about writing. Rake said he could see no reason for trying it, since good work is painful to accomplish. "I like nonsense, though," he added. "I write very good nonsense."

The fire burned low in its charred framework, and Rake's eyes were in black hollows so I could not tell whether he really looked at me or not. And it was important to know.

Today the sea sounds, but not aloud.

If Philip does not come soon —

I shall stop now. When Rake rouses himself we shall have lunch and go to Blackwall. Perhaps I shall hear from Philip. I recognize this as one of those recurrent times in my life when trouble grows like a branch.

June 8 — Yesterday in Blackwall Rake found a check at the post office, something that he gets each month from his father's small estate. And I had a letter from Philip. He cannot come here, for he has no funds; at least not now, but he is in Toledo awaiting payment for the sale of a picture. In the spring he sold it to a wealthy woman.

I hastened along the street to find Rake, and we bought alcohol and supplies. Drinking coffee in The Spotlight, I read Philip's letter again, as I would read a story in a magazine: *You see, Judith, I have but ten dollars. This would no doubt get me to you, but there I would be confronted with a life of running rings around the figure zero, biting off little pieces from time to time as nourishment. . . . I want so much to be with you — more — to adore you — and forget such matters as the sale of pictures — it is so stupid to find oneself on hands and knees to Materialism.*

We started back to Salt House in the liberal light of early afternoon, which lay laced in among the leaves of the trees and bushes in the woods. We stopped at the gin tree a moment for drinks, and then, walking together, with the gunnysacks over our shoulders, I was thinking, "Since you are beside me, this path is as it never was, or ever can be hereafter."

When we climbed up into the dunes, the light, no longer caught in nets of trees, veneered out over all the rounding hills. It seemed to be actually moving along with us, because we were so talkative and free. When the sun is no more than the limelight in which we bask, there is, I must say, a vanity in our happiness! Rake looked up just in time to see a gull standing still on the high air, at full tilt, but didn't say a word about it.

We left the light and went into the house. I looked across the rooms to the sea, which shows through the open north door like a piece of blue paper pasted down and, for further security, barred across with the irregular sloping of a dune. Whenever I enter, I look there; in that tall narrow frame at the end of the little hall it has the clear simplicity of a Japanese print, and when there is a storm and the door is closed, I feel dangerously shut in, and the house seems blinded. I rely a great deal on that door's being open.

What shall I say about Salt House — isolated as a ship, and silent, with the living silence of an audience, though at the same time filled with the unceasing fluid articulation of the sea. I want to say something important about it — that it has an insistence to drama exactly in the way that with this clutter of ours, these cigarette butts, dirty beer bottles, scattered papers, unwashed dishes, and faded flowers, each object stands out in the manner of an arranged and painted still-life. Even the clock lends itself to the illusion, for it has no minute hand. The commonplace is defeated here, as I have seen it defeated nowhere else except upon the stage. And there it is defeated by artful exclusions; here by I know not what strangeness. Once across the dunes we live in an exquisite unreality.

June 9 — But what I meant to write down was simply that Feargus and a stripling named Martin were in the kitchen. Martin is Rake's friend, thin, with a witty face and some mysterious kind of bitterness which will never solidify, just as his body will never thicken.

"Where you been?" asked Rake. "Meet Judith."

"Hello," I said. "Won't you stay to supper? We've got things to eat."

"I've been downtown buying poison," Martin said in a racing voice. "I told the clerk in the drugstore, 'Give me anything good for killing parents.'"

"Well," I said, putting the food into the pantry, "the police won't come way out here after you. Feargus, go on — pour us a drink."

We sat around in the kitchen having a beer, and then the two boys went up to clear the sea chambers of flies. They've been coming in through the pane I had to smash. Martin speared them with scissors, taking the postures of a fencer, and Rake snapped his fists on them. I sat on the windowsill, laughing at these antics, and the sun flooded in richly.

Below on the shore, the old wrecked boiler, and winches and pipes from a buried schooner, continually broke up the water that poured over them. In the north the sea was a pool of light, with blots of stillness spread over the everlasting agitation. Far out there lay a bank of fog; we heard the buoy ringing, or blowing, rather, its dull short-throated clangor.

The pool lengthened into a path, into whose apex the sun sank with demure ease.

Settling down, we lit cigarettes and approached not even warily the torrents of evening talk to come.

Then I went out with Martin, and we sat on our heels at the foot of a slope and kept digging with long swipes across a section of sand, so that the top grains were set streaming down in an ordering flow, and although our eyes were not quick enough to follow the subterranean motion, we saw a strange internal flux beneath the surface. We were enthusiastic about this play, and this alone, and we were children in this and no more than children, and both together knew the sea behind us was clean, the bank above us was clean-cut against the sky, and I thought to myself — and it was flowing under the fresh and simple pleasure in a larger, deeper motion like the sand — "Maybe we can share this play and yet each have it separately, and let it alone."

Dinner was our feast, but Martin was ill and moaned, "I want to drink, but when I drink I die, and die, and die!" He went out to escape the warm smoke and fishy odors of the kitchen, and stretched weeping upon the sand. He was weeping for a girl who had died, and kept calling out, "Ann, Ann — Mary Ann," over and over again.

"He is a creature so sensitive," Feargus explained to us, "that he feels first with antennae what we others have to learn with coarser organs. I'll venture he knows even now what we say of him."

When he went to fetch Martin in by the fireplace, Rake winked at me across the table. "Feargus has antennae, too," he said, "his ears!"

So Rake knows, too, that sly post behind the pantry door, where that heavy fox stands when you think him asleep, and turns away unabashed, without scurrying, if you choose to discover him there.

How much I have written today! My hand aches, but there is still more for the record.

Feargus laid his body that was flooded with comforts on the blue divan, and the boys lay on the hearth singing blatantly.

Once I left them, to read again from my letter. This is part of what Philip wrote: *To hell with long, soft June evenings, under present circumstances a definite source of annoyance. Annihilate them with a word or perhaps a gesture of the hand — use another word, change the gesture — ah, they refuse to be annihilated.*

A world staring at two round black pieces of glass.

He has pink eye!

He is being fitted for nose glasses.

Much better that way. Let them not know that he, the romanticist, walked in moonlight, walked in the shadow of a rose arbor, that the surface of his eye was scratched by a thorn hanging in the shadow.

Now the black glasses are discarded, everything is as it was before — but he has been punished. To hell with June evenings. Annihilate them with a word, a gesture —

I sit drinking chicken-feed wine made by Feargus's recipe. I am able to think only of you, of Feargus, of the sound of water washing over sand. The curious, wholly individualistic taste of the wine makes it impossible to disassociate it from thoughts of night at Salt House.

I paced up and down in the darkness beyond the firelight for a long time. The driftwood was festooned with seaweed, and thus the fire seemed like a little shaggy house. Feargus stirred with anger; he wanted to tell his stories — that I knew — but I felt stubborn. I was holding all the strings of the occasion, and youth should have its little hour! What I was really thinking was how distasteful this inaccurate noise would be to Philip if he were here.

If he were here!

They reached war songs finally, but after a few phrases they faltered.

"'Put your head down, Fritzy boy!' — how could they sing it?" said Rake in a sober voice. "Judith, you were old enough to see something of the war; you were lucky. And to see how people felt about it."

"I didn't understand, though," I replied. "And everyone was ignorant then, except the responsible ones. Besides, I was young then, even younger than you are now." I laughed. "Well, I can't afford to brood over *that!*" and went on, "You know, in Germany last year, a man told me he and his friends would run away, to Denmark or anywhere, if another war threatened them. 'It iss awful, it iss awful,' he told me, showing me photographs. Singularly, his pictures were mostly of officers' funerals: altars piled with paper flowers, and other officers standing beside the coffins."

"It won't be Denmark, but jail for us," remarked Martin, brightly ominous.

"Jail for an idea isn't so bad," Rake declared, and lest he had gone too far out of his professed futilities he yawned as he said it. "As good as any other place, I guess. You can sleep and eat; what else do you want?"

"You can't make love," Martin darted at him.

"Hm-m."

I find that is his most frequent noncommittal reply.

"Well," I took it up, "there's a feverish perverse kind of joy which can't be taken away from you, if you're jailed for an idea. The *idea* is your love."

"I said *make* love," responded Martin shortly, and Rake sounded again his awkward "Hm-m."

Feargus, who had been snoring, now grunted, "'God hates a coward' is a classic of the cattle country now all but gone," and tottered bulkily out into the boiling room to bed.

"We should talk," Rake said after a few moments, as he poured out another scud of beer into the pitcher. "We've none of us tried holding out against anything."

Martin took up the challenge. "I was kicked out of college," he said grimly.

"And I was divorced," I exclaimed, without gaiety.

Rake stirred. "And I refuse to work." Suddenly we all shouted with laughter, and all talked at once, saying, "So here we are — just where we want to be! It's easy, after all."

The night deepened. The box seats on either side of the hearth make an alcove, and we leaned against these. Rake was sitting on a pile of driftwood, but as the fire grew darker he slipped down and lay like a dog on the floor. Sometimes our hands wavered out for our crocks of beer.

Martin pulled a slip of newspaper from his pocket and threw a brittle old branch on the fire for light. "'I hardly believe,'" he read, "'that anyone can really fall in love who does not know some poetry by heart . . . or face dying . . . or enjoy anything — sunrise, the sea, forests, moonlight — without tunes in his head . . .'"

I shouted this down and angered him. He cried back, "Poetry is more necessary than bread or water!" and I, in turn, cried that I would smash his rosy glasses, that in the deepest moments one *feels*, one does not quote.

"I'm damned certain I shall live by poetry, though."

"All right, in a dream world, then," I answered. "As for me, I want what is true and real."

"A dream world? Good!" he mused. "Listen, I wrote a poem all about the fictitious value of time. It said that the Greek statue has really no greater degree of beauty, because it is built for centuries, than the flower that blooms and drops within a day."

"Yes, but — " Rake and I called out together, each blocking the other and forgetting what we were going to say. Then Rake remembered. "Time *has* a beauty value," he stated. "It enriches things, even the simplest things. . . . But we sound like a goddamn bunch of Bohemians."

"I'm not; I'm a Buddhist, because I've got trouble with my umbilicus," Martin proclaimed.

"And as for you," murmured Rake at my elbow, "my, but you're serious, and of such a moral persuasion! There's no doing anything with you." I felt his lips grazing ever so timidly the inside of my forearm. And almost at the same time Martin caught my hand on the other side. He was opposite me, and our outstretched arms just touched across the space of rug.

"She's a Greek, and tonight she belongs to us," he said. I could feel Rake moving nearer, and finally his head pressed down into my lap. We all fell silent in this sleepy, remote, and faintly vibrant embrace, and didn't talk or stir any more until the windows blued, and the massive chairs and tables came swimming milkily into sight.

Something about dawn came into our heads, and we staggered out the north door and down the beach. I coiled miserably in a hollow of the bank while the two boys watched the thick damp clouds. We found our expedition ridiculous and walked back to Salt House. Feargus was up and had made toast and coffee, which we needed, for we were shaking with fatigue and chill.

"I'll raise the sun for you prodigals," he boasted. "Wait, I'll get into my costume of the sun-worshiper. I'll fling my arms from the tops of the hills and give a Persian cry, and then I shall be strong all day."

When he came again into the kitchen we lifted our eyelids heavily to gaze, for below the mottled pink chest, the white belly, was tied a strip of fawn-colored rag.

"Oh, good! Very good!" we encouraged him, with nodding heads. He strode out, and immediately after an oriental glow stained the walls. We plunged out the south door, and there on the promontory was Feargus with the flap of his loin cloth lifted, and spray blowing away on the early wind, although he was directing it at the very center of the sunrise. Hearing us, he whipped around with a growl.

We rushed into the house, and we separately found beds and flung ourselves down with our mouths still twitching with smiles.

Now it is ten o'clock in the morning. I am lying in the sea chamber, still alone. I have wakened only long enough to reach out to the driftwood plank by the bedside for my journal, and to write what I remember of yesterday.

Continuously, beneath speech, I know two things: that I should stop what is happening here with Rake, and that I cannot.

Just now, after I wrote the last words, the wind streaming in through the broken pane turned the pages of this journal back to an entry of the winter: *And yet she is weary of dreaming alone. When will he come? Where is it he lingers? He will return to her, she knows he will return.*

But I am not perplexed, and directly I shall fall asleep. I have given my heart the direction.

June 10 — Dusky red moon, red as black cherry wine or a watermelon, we couldn't tell which.

June 12 — Wet rain out of a wet sky falling on the wet ground. The rain stopped, the sun came out, and suddenly the whole face of the dunes changed, and it was as if somehow, unexpectedly, they had been left a fortune.

We have been drinking for three days. Certainly my last entries here are a brief betrayal of some sort of impressionistic excitement. (I had to erase some of them!) While it rained, we strolled about the house or stretched out on the blue divan in the storage room. Every time the clock struck, that clock without a minute hand, we looked at one another hopelessly. We were weak from drinking, and yet only waited till night to begin again. We were like passengers waiting in a railroad station where trains whistle by mournfully but never stop for us.

This afternoon, at last, I am sober. It no longer rains, but the sky is gray and thick as a blotter. After I wash the dishes at the pump in the pantry we are going to Blackwall — Rake, Martin, and I, because we feel the superiority of underdogs, and we need food.

June 14 — I meant to stay faithful to Philip, and I can hardly believe that it has happened otherwise. When I think of the last two years, then of our many letters that planned a life together — and now *this!* But Rake was tantalizing, with his mockery of everything in the world. I had to see him subdued.

It began under the lighthouse. I couldn't resist his touch when he became bold at last. We went falling down over the Clay Pounds to the dark safe shore.[7] Afterward we swam in the strange surf we had never seen by day, and a column of white fire, the moon it was, was burning behind clouds low against the horizon. Then we climbed up the Pounds. First he tried to pull me down to the shore again, but I couldn't seem to return, and we kept slipping and clutching at the ribbons of grass. We drove back toward Blackwall, still pressed close together, in the stolen car, going wildly over the black hills of Dangerfield, with dawn at the end. We slept, finally, in Rake's camp.

But I am too anxious to write this down, as if it would relieve me of guilt. (I am determined not to feel guilt.) I must go back and tell the rest.

Early in the evening we three crossed the dunes. It was warm and windy, and we seemed to go along, amiably hand in hand, over the Hitch in great leaps. Then we swung through the town, hurrying along the waterfront street, our rubber raincoats ballooning out behind us. The evening came in yellow, with a sullen dead color that spread over the whole sky and made clay of the harbor water. All the mackerel fleet was in, which meant a storm. The masts dipped and rose, windy and troubled; the moist shore was empty of life, and all along the highwater line were dead fish, their white bellies turned up and all their mouths strained open in the same anguished way, so that one almost heard the fishy scream.

We tried to get into a Knights of Columbus dance, but they put us out because we were barefooted. A man who was standing in the doorway followed us and invited us to his place. He was an engineer at work on the new road out to the sea, and, like so many people who come to Blackwall, he had a studio. Tonight he wanted to talk to someone about his experiences in the war, and he plied us with whisky of undeniable quality, in order to make us listen.

The boys were uneasy and, from behind his back, made signals toward the door. But I didn't want to go away; I wanted to see them bait him. He was a practical and brutal man. He had covered the big studio window with bluebird cretonne and put in Grand Rapids rocking chairs and lamps with pink pagoda shades.

"I need to come out of here," he said. "It makes me think of artists."

"Why did you rent it, then?"

"Wonderful for parties," he smirked.

In the kitchenette Rake suddenly pushed him in the chest so that he sat down hastily on a bench, and then standing over him began talking loudly and furiously. "So you want another war? So you think it's great stuff? Well, you may think you'll get us kids out for it, but let me tell you, mister, you won't! We heard about the cock-eyed stinking mess."

Martin got around behind the engineer's back and waggled his fingers at me frantically. I grinned, because I had caught Rake in some strong feeling at last, actually in a *parti pris,* and also because the man on the bench looked bewildered. But there was a red and alcoholic gleam in his eyes I didn't like. "Rake, we have to go," I said, and pulled on my sweater. It was nearly morning. We skulked out because we had been drinking his good whisky while not liking him.

Once safely on the back street we danced along until nearly out of town, when we decided to take Amanda Meredith's car and drive to the lighthouse. Amanda is Rake's aunt. Martin, however, wanted to sleep, as well as see his mail, which has been collecting for days, and we left him at his boarding house door.

The top of the lighthouse was a nugget of metal and glass, its four bars of light swinging upon us every seventh second, and beyond it the stars seemed only a dim experimental stencil.

The rest of the night I have told already.

Toward noon we wakened in the camp. There was no water for priming the pump, and no food except dry bread. Beyond the pines was a gravel banking, thick with little yellow flowers of the poverty grass, which daily fall in myriads and daily grow as many more. I lay there at full length for a while, face down, seeing their petals at eye level, letting the dry stems scratch my arms like spiders, and scaling interest down to the degree of leaf and pebble, which was truly restful.

As we crossed the dunes in the flat depressive light of noon, we saw many of these lakes of yellow flowers. Our path toward Salt House (and toward Feargus — would he know? would he be surprised?) drew us through the buried forest, where branches hard and naked as bone stood out of the sand. Mackerel gulls screamed not far above, almost beating our heads with their feet, for this is where they lay their eggs. (I wish I could find one!)

And now I am truly aroused, recording, satisfied.

June 15 — Sunday. Rain.

Last night we slept on the floor by the fire, but the cricket behind the panel kept me awake. At last I left Rake on the divan and went back to my own bed in the sea chamber. We have not been drinking, and now he is embarrassed — no, something other than that. I dare not touch him, and he pretends nothing has happened. Almost I would say he has been precocious in love, and something unfortunate happened which filled him with confusion, if not fear.

Yet, when we walked up the shore toward the sunset last night, and I tried to say that, he pinched my arm. "What you don't realize," he said, "is just that you're complicated about everything, and I'm very simple."

We are alone in the house and had lunch alone, for Feargus has withdrawn himself. A quart of alcohol, which we have been trying to make palatable with orange peels, has also disappeared.

As soon as I finish this we are going to put on raincoats and cut through the wet beach grass to the Interpreter's House, there to pacify him by asking for the blessing which he likes so much to give. Ah, Feargus — a little sulky because your mischief worked so well?

Rake must beat his way down to New York, for he has to talk over the plots for his "true" stories with an editor before he is allowed to do them. I'm only going into Blackwall. To further ingratiate ourselves with the Interpreter we will pour a few drinks into the bottle in the gin tree.

June 19 — That day we found Martin in bed with a swarm of books and papers tumbling off his jacked-up knees. "Why don't you do 'true' stories and make some money?" Rake suggested. "Instead of that stuff. I'll teach you the formula: it's sin, suffer, repent, and reform."

"Only if I'm allowed to reverse the order," returned Martin, and we tried it out in chorus: "Reform, repent, suffer, *s-s-sin*!"

"Let's go along to New York with Rake!" I proposed to Martin, and then there we were: three figures walking in the rain, one reading aloud *The Primer of Aesthetics*, the two hilarious.[8] Three in the back seat of one car after another, making fantastic replies to patronizing questions — three wandering toward New York in the rain.

Fishermen in a brisk new car give us a lift and draughts of prune whisky like flavored raw alcohol. We promise to go on a fishing trip with them soon.

Coffee, frankfurters, and beans at the Canal, and we linger over them, basking in the warmth, and sleepy.[9] The line of electric lights, lashed to poles on the water, are footlights before the shore's dark stage.

The road becomes simply a moving belt, detached, not really touching the countryside at all. Then a rhythmic progression: pointing, the back seat, riding two miles, ten miles, thirty miles, descending and pointing again.[10] Until it was night in Rhode Island, and a voice lingered to say, "Kids, you better watch out for Chrysler Imperials — the police — better flag only Connecticut cars." Cars pass at midnight with certainly no rides for suspicious characters, bandits in bedraggled clothes, bandanna on a girl's neck, the boys unshaved.

Resting in a grove, smoking and singing blues. No rides, and we understand, yes, we *become* enemies of society. We swagger. Our voices are coarse with exuberance; we have poverty — my God! how nice that is for a little while. We spring into the lights that come flowing over the road bed, and thumb our noses and raucously shout *Bourgeois!* or *Allons, Enfants de la Patrie,* or, as irreverantly as possible, we chant *Ten Cents a Dance.*

Two traveling salesmen are lonely as far as Meriden. We sink in a row upon the back seat; when they come to the crisis of each shameless story, the boys sing out *Tra-la-lala-la-lula-lula!* lest I hear. This is The Road; it is dangerous.

The riders of the night are truckmen. Above a load we lie prone, on our faces, swaying high in air and belabored by the rain. Cities and towns, filling stations lurid as vaudeville, how splendid they are: lately new, broken sharp, with a luster, out of the block of darkness.

"Swell!" I gesticulate toward Socony and Colonial.[11]

"Tawdry!" accuses Martin. "Tawdry is a word from the fair of St. Audrey where giddy trinkets were sold. I looked it up in the dictionary."

"No, not that, not really that." I will not speak any more my pleasure almost furtive, and suddenly it comes to mind that another boy, ungainly and young as Rake, once asked in a tearoom, "Do you like beauty?" and I said, "O dear! You must never ask people that — only surgeons are allowed such intimacy."

We three hold hands, our voices call back and forth above the shivering roar.

Once we pass a restaurant whose name in diamond lights is Roaderia.

Coffee again, behind streaming windowpanes, in warmth of blue gas flames, copper, and blazing enameled walls. The driver, pasty with exhaustion, falls asleep across his wheel, and we crawl into another truck, a regular barracks.

"Let's set up housekeeping in here!" We roll in musty quilts. When underway, I find Rake's hands groping to enclose mine, his cheek close against my face. Strange sleep: the driver's face in the small window now and then, and alternate lights and darkness, long pauses of the motor that waken us, and we breathe restlessly.

In the morning the driver turned us out at Ninth Avenue and Fourteenth Street.

I think of Philip's brother. He, Waverley Hatefield, will give us hot water, towels, morning coffee; he will rejoice at the unexpected, the courageous. I am confident of this because he, too, has lived at Salt House, and because of Philip, who will soon be there.

Failure — too early intruded. We enter, sit, and he stares at us. Through his eyes we look out and see ourselves childish, boorish. He, handsome as a doll, hands in the pockets of a green flannel dressing gown, cigarette at a quizzical angle — he has done this for us. We shuffle out, no longer amused or proud of our plight.

Long Island City, but I shall never recall crossing the bridge. Doors open and close; I sink into a bed still warm as a pocket from someone else's sleep. Sleep then, weak and nervous, like being chained to the bed. Waking and opening the door, I found a disheveled home. A girl named Trixie was embroidering. She said she would make coffee, but added doubtfully that was all she could do. Apparently someone who had gone out had instructed her to say this. We talked together as two women; in fact, in another moment we would have been arranging each other's hair, if Rake and Martin had not appeared. They brought sardines, bologna, French bread, mustard, cheese, and fruit, which they piled on the table over the litter of a previous meal.

Everything in the kitchen was covered with dirty dishes, even a corner of the floor. There were ferns, a radio, Maxfield Parrish pictures. Sometimes foreign people came in, or simply stood in the doorways with their hats on, looking at us. The master of this household has gone away in his toga and sandals. He made salt in the garage and is taking it to India.

New York again. On the Cameo screen senators talked about prohibition, and when the newsreel rooster flapped his wings, we exclaimed, "It's the birdie!"

We went for a ride in a taxi and screamed in unison to startle people on the street, but they paid very little attention. We walked, chanting, "I'm going mad, stark staring mad!" but no one noticed except a policeman, who told us to shut up.

Then we went to see *Uncle Vanya,* and when the curtain fell after the lines *And those who, in this existence, didn't love us, they'll love us . . . they'll want us . . . ,* wherein we fled each other into our separate lives in memory, we went into the streets again.[12]

Time for more food, this time Chinese. A policeman snorted, "Artists!" as we limped past, and we threw kisses back at him, which turned to the classic gesture of derision. We couldn't find any of our friends, and, while sitting on some steps on Tenth Street, were showered with cold water. An angry voice fell upon us as we dashed into the street. At the same time, a man rushed out from a speakeasy and heaved an empty gallon tin at Martin, shouting, "Communists!" as he disappeared around the corner. We decided to leave New York.

I found a friend, and she was kind, giving me a cot, allowing the boys to sleep on the floor.

It went on. Rake got his plots in hand, while I took Martin to an alcoholic tea party. Our appearance was uncouth, but our vivacity disarming — at least *we* thought so.

The trucks at twilight loomed and swept round the corner of Tenth Avenue and Fourteenth Street. This was the least moment; this was the time when the journey seemed long and cold. A man stopped, took us all up in the front seat with him. He was a robustly big man and pulled deeply at the whisky we gave him. When we asked his name he said, "Call me John." Going along the Concourse he leans far out, whistling to girls and singing. I see the abundant life of warm evening in the Bronx, motion relaxed and vital on curbs and in doorways.

John says he was a top-sergeant, and America won the war. He climbs out for a drink at the edge of a park, and about nine o'clock he wants to stop and dance. I am afraid to refuse. Martin wants to protect me in some way, and before I can stop him, he says I am his wife. John's pride is seriously damaged by the very simplicity of this attempt at deception, and now he is going to punish us. In a dark place, with woods on either side, he stops the truck and bids us climb out. There, close to the truck's shadow he starts fighting with the boys, and they do not believe in fighting. They keep their hands down and I circle about fearfully, wondering if they'll both be knocked out, and if, after all, principle is more important than me! Gloatingly I decide that it is, yet I'm bashing his head all the time with my walking stick.

"You're a liar," he roars at Martin, and slaps him open-handed again and again. Martin is so angry that he won't even step out of range, while Rake keeps jumping aside and arguing, "Come on, bozo! We don't fight, see?"

John turns on me. "*You'll* fight, you little devil, anyway!" and he wrests the stick from me and snaps it over his knee. It's no use, and tears of exasperation spring to my eyes. He represents something we don't understand. The Road again!

What comes into his head? He orders us back into the truck and we obey. As I sit on Martin's lap, I feel how he trembles with his hatred of the strength of the top-sergeant. Rake takes the wheel, and John falls across my back, snoring. All night we go, but whenever Rake asks directions the driver is incoherent, and when morning whitens we are going into Springfield, miles out of our path. The beast on my back stretches, groans, and takes the wheel. He drops me off at a corner.

"Listen, the company wouldn't like me driving in with a girl, see? I'll leave the boys in a garage, and we'll come back for you later."

I'm so sleepy that it never occurs to me to wonder why I can't go to the garage, too. Meekly I sit down in a doorway, and drop my head between my knees, while the early red dust of a good day filters over the street.

Later, there is John alone, walking, a suitcase in his hand. "I got to deliver some liquor to a friend, hush-like," he says. "Going to meet him in his garage. So follow me, but don't make no noise."

We skirt a church, and he helps me over a picket fence at the back. I'm uneasy.

"Can't I wait outside and smoke a cigarette?" I ask, as we approach the garage.

"Say, kid, are you scared or something? You *got* to come in. I told you this was hush, didn't I? If his wife looks out the window she'd see you. And I don't want to get him into no trouble."

Suddenly in a sharp voice I ask, "What are you locking the doors for?"

"For Christ's sake, what you so nervous about? I thought you was a sport." Now I am certain of trouble. His tone of impersonal reasonableness has changed to wheedling. Where are Rake and Martin?

"Get in the car and be comfortable. You didn't get much sleep last night." His voice is syrup.

"Not with you lolloping over my back, I didn't," I say bitterly, standing near the door. "And if you've got any funny business in mind, I'll yell like a siren."

"Get in the car! I ain't done nothing yet, have I? What you squealing about? Some sport, you are!"

That's right; no use yelling when nothing has happened. The newspaper phrase flashes into my mind, and "No story!" I say grimly as I climb into the front seat of the sedan. This is a mistake; it gives him his cue, and he is on me, lifting and pushing me toward the back seat. But he is in front of me, and I reach around the hot bulk of his shoulder and press the button of the horn.

"Quit that, you goddamned bitch!" and I get a clout on the side of the head. Why don't I scream? I burst into tears instead. "Oh, please, let me alone. Don't slap my face. I hate to have my face slapped. Please. I didn't mean to cry, but I can't help it."

"Jesus! Don't cry. Let's get out of here, only don't cry. You got a handkerchief? I got one, but it's dirty."

I nod, wrenching at my bandana, and he climbs out of the car and unlocks the doors. To my surprise we drive out of the yard with aplomb and down the street. It must have been his own car all the time.

Outside the city we stop at a barber shop, and there are Rake and Martin. When, reunited, we see the last of his sullen back, we burst into song. We remain young and innocent — if we are worth anything at all, we are remaining young and innocent!

Now we have to sleep. A baker's cart carries us into the country. Below a wooded slope he drops us off, leaving a loaf of bread. Our money is almost gone, and we have a long way to go today.

We climb the hill and nudge down into the pine needles. Across the road is a river lying flat and glassy among thickets and plumose elm trees, from which are rising the mists of early morning. One waking glance I turn upon Rake. There is power in us, and no doubt we can go around the world. We live by our wits, we are charming, a baker has given us a loaf of bread to tear with our fingers. Sleep, my wastrels, my sons, my comrades.

Wakened by the sounds of midday, we shout down at The Road and lift our throats to the last of the whisky. Only trucks stop for us today, small ones, not the mammoths of the night.

Wherever we see a "No Loitering" sign, it is there we loiter.

On a village green we lie outstretched, eating ham sandwiches.

A white church crowns the hill, points into a picture postcard blue and white sky.

"Hey, kid, what's the name of this place?"

Two State policemen drive up and, with notebooks in hand, curtly ask me if my parents know I am on The Road? I tell them I am twenty-eight years old.

"How much money have you?" they ask the boys.

"Sixty cents."

We are courteous, our manner is positively distinguished; they tip their caps and drive away.

Somehow we get into Rhode Island again. In a mill yard the boys help load great rolls of candy-box paper, dresden roses, and scarlet tinsel into a truck, while I bring cups of water from the steam-pressure room. Coal cinders in the yard burn through the soles of my shoes. The day wears thin with heat.

Martin climbs up with the driver, while Rake and I are stowed on a shelf of the paper rolls, just under the roof. As the countryside pours out behind us, we talk about being young, and then about being dead. Rake makes a slight motion so that my hand is touching his shoulder, and we don't talk.

The truck jams still, and Martin is below, shouting up at us. "We're going the wrong way. Jump out, before the lights change — *quickly!*" he cries. We throw our raincoats out into the street and leap down, just as the truck swings away. We stand confused, Rake and I still flushed from the delicate proximity. A small crowd has gathered, curious and inimical. This is Woonsocket. We walk for miles. The people on the streets are French mill workers and regard us with suspicion. Two men in an older car say they will take us for a ride as soon as they've picked up some more friends. That doesn't seem inviting, and I don't like the way they look at me and chuckle to each other. We go into a store, having malted milks and crackers, and linger there until there's no longer any chance of meeting them.

"If we slick up, maybe we'll get better rides," we agree. And we wash carefully, and Martin even goes so far as to buy a comb. This leaves us but nine cents.

At twilight we are still walking. We had better spend the nine cents. Resting under a tree we talk it over and decide to buy two ice cream cones, charging the penny. Martin goes across to a roadside stand, waggling his backside, tipping his hat to passing cars, and finagles the two cones. But Rake, about to taste the cream thirstily, suddenly slaps his thigh.

"What! No cigarettes?"

Again Martin clowns his way across the road and exchanges the cones for a short package of Luckies.

Night falls. We mean to reach Blackwall without delay. At last, at a signpost, a doctor picks us up in a great blue roadster. At Foxboro we wait again and declare in desperation that we will ride with anyone, anywhere, except back to New York. Two young school teachers, amazed, carry us to the corner where traffic turns off for Blackwall. We stand near an unlighted house. No rain, no heat, but a sticky choking fog moving low along the ground. I can smell the bruised succulence of geranium leaves somewhere near.

Stamping our feet against the chill, we sing once more:

> I went down to St. James's Infirmary
> And found my baby there,

Stretched out on a long white table —
So young, so cold, so bare . . .

But we are tired. On this trip we have whittled one another's minds down to sharp points, but they blunt again in hunger and discouragement. "Hell!" says Martin. "I'm not a good talker. I can't explain what I mean about things, but I go around giving clues."

A fast car passes, slows, and in the red glow of the taillight we rush upon it. A man, huddled in a fur coat, points with his thumb at the back seat and there we sink down, wordlessly, arms and legs entangled for warmth.

Rake's lips touched my ear. "I'm afraid I'm cock-eyed about you."

"I'll go to the camp tomorrow night," I whispered boldly in return. I hadn't been sure about him, even after the lighthouse, but I was sure now.

Martin moaned and turned away. Oh, why did I have to go dashing at things this way? Had I no reticence? Confidently Rake's head lay in the hollow under my shoulder, and his hands touched my throat. Thus we fell asleep.

At Temple the silent man turned us out, and we stood at the four corners where the lights burned red — amber — green, over and over, but no cars passed under them. Mosquitoes swarmed in the malarial fog. We planned drearily to start walking to Blackwall, and stumbled along for fifteen miles in a dream awake.

Faintly, I know that alone — for Rake and Martin dropped off in town — I fell asleep on the highest dune, over whose crest drove a gale from the sea and where no mosquitoes could cling. And in the ruddy dawn light I staggered along the Salt House Hitch.

Feargus, when he found me here again, gave me coffee and food, saying, "My children did well to make a demonstration for Communism. I'm glad I sent you out in the world."

"But that wasn't it. We went because we had been drinking together, and simply didn't want to separate. We weren't Communists; we were bums."

"What rejoices me," he explained, "is that they threw a tin can and a bucket of water at you, because they saw mischief. It proves to me that New York has become at last Communist conscious!"

When I close my eyes I see The Road swooping and diving before me like a fantastic river. I *am* so tired.

After sunset I am going to slip out, by way of the tower, and go to the camp.

Philip has had nothing to do with all this. I long for the certainty he will bring. And the quiet. If I went away from him on this trip, I have now, in Salt House, returned.

June 20 — I went to town for a sackful of supplies, then through the wood by the Whistle Trail, which comes out on the dunes near the camp. The sunset was saffron, lying low under bulging gray clouds. At the dip of the trail I looked back over my shoulder and saw the storm signals hung out in dull murderous red above Monument Hill.[13]

Rake was not there. I spread the damp blankets over small pine trees in a clearing, made some supper, and crawled into the tent. Until darkness I watched the skyline of the trail, then tried to sleep. Whenever a branch brushed against the tent, I thought it was his step and became very nervous.

All night I lay there, sleeping a little and listening long to the rising wind. Drops of moisture, shaken down from the trees, gathered to fall from the tent ropes. I think there was a moon behind the fog, for the dunes lay in luminous pallor.

Again at dawn I dragged over the sand to Salt House.

June 21 — At noon, while I was writing, Rake arrived. We had both lunched but went out on the tower platform with a bottle of beer and felt upheld by all the horizons. He said his uncle kept him in town, nor did he think I would remember the camp or want to stay there in such weather.

June 22 — Now I am certain of him. He has been with me for twenty-four hours, and he has even used the difficult expression, *I love you.*

"I love you!" entranced, exhausted. And, young man, I know you will elude me, that I have you only on the wing. You said, in the sea chamber, kneeling beside my chair, head turned away, "You're a swell bozo, Judith. This is the first time this has happened — I thought it was serious before, but it wasn't like this. This is really serious."

The long sweet afternoon passed away. Sometimes we talked.

"Philip is coming here as soon as he gets some money. Last year we committed ourselves to this, and it is true that I love him."

We both stir uneasily, and Rake turns his face into the pillow. I know the secret retreat; how often have I, beyond weeping, but shuddering, burrowed into my own self, and found my own self there like another person.

"Hm-m," Rake mutters; then we embrace like two children. "I guess I'll go away soon."

"No!"

We heard the surf beginning to crash on the outer bar, which meant that the tide had turned to drive in again, and it sounded like the rattling of chains.

Downstairs we heard the stealthy tread of Feargus. I thought of how he had asked me, following the footprints, to be kind to Rake, and I realized, perhaps clearly for the first time, that he loves mischief as dearly as anything in the world.

"Listen to Feargus, the clumsy pard, down there," I said. "He suspects no one will cook his supper tonight."

"Let's neglect him. We coddle him too much for his own good sometimes, don't you think? He's like our baby!"

The light of day burned down, and the slow gray shadow of twilight settled upon the air like sifting ash. Now we heard only the fringe and spill of the flood tide. Blue smoke from our cigarettes rose in a double stalk of calla lilies that broke, wove back, entwined.

June 23 — Voices rise up the companionway from the kitchen, where my guests are drinking. After breakfast this morning Rake sat at the Corona, saying, "Let's write poems. Say something and then keep rhyming it." He started off with:

> His eyes were bulged,
> His mouth was taut,
> His coat was flying aft —
> Be ne'er may the soul of a man be bought

Who floats to sea on a raft.

"Now, Judith, give us some feminine poetry, give us something womanly."

I recited a collection of tenuous words:

The sun and moon and stars conspire,
But clarity is never there;
As mist obscures their rise and wane
So impotent the personal blood
To explicate the pain.

Martin turned away. "Listen, Judith. Can I use your sea chamber for work while you're in Blackwall?"

"Yes," I said. "It belongs to you this instant, and until noon."

When I came back, I found a sonnet on the desk, though Martin was fast asleep on the blue divan. The sonnet was to "Ann, Ann, Mary Ann."

I brought a new young man back with me, a schoolboy with a model curly head, at present too large for his body. He has arrogance rather than bitterness, so Rake and Martin don't like him. Sometimes I hear a scuffling and they thrust him out, locking the door, but Max is stubborn. He goes up the roof to the tower, climbs down the ladder, and without apology flies through my door and downstairs.

Philip, when will you be here?

Now they are raising a din about poetry again. I ran down a moment ago to criticize Martin's sonnet figure of scarlet flowers. "But that is a translation of emotion," he explains.

"Well, they're quite nice here, in your sonnet, but I must say in general the trouble is the roses aren't fresh new flowers, but like musty velvet ones off an old hat."

At this they started throwing bottles at me, and now they are in the Come to Jesus stage, all except Martin, who keeps putting his head in the companionway and shouting confusedly, "If only art survives, if only art survives!"

Feargus, jealous of their potency, likes to encourage young men to drink. (Perhaps the only trouble is that I'm sober!)

Later —The simpler things at Salt House do not now engross me as they did in other years. The lights are still moving along the dark verges of the sea; if the wind is landward, I still hear the slow *cling-cling* of the buoy, and the water beats back and forth with the same sounds — sometimes they are plunging and deep, and sometimes only a furling wash, but always sounding, even though our ears, attuned, forget to listen. I remember how, alone, I read by lamplight, and how I paced the shore. The stars spelled out one idea or another, the sea steadied me with its great voiceless reminding that beauty is not young, and where the alluvial gravel lies back in a hollow I used to stand, tall as a stalk in the waste, and speak aloud:

> Sophocles long ago
> Heard it on the Aegean, and it brought
> Into his mind . . .

But now, instead of all that fostered, almost precious eagerness, I talk, plan, write, and drink, and my nights are not lonely. At this moment Rake is asleep in my bed, and from the desk I look across the room at him. One hand is thrust into his hair, the other relaxed flat upon the pillow. I would like to understand him, but despite the supple engine of his body, he chooses to be ungainly and inarticulate. Is it any wonder that I am less concerned than formerly with the passing lights at sea?

June 24 — Sunday. This morning the house and food became my own. Perhaps the need was concocted out of weariness; I found that I wanted the walls bared, the sills of the windows cleared so that once more they coupled themselves to the horizon. As soon as Rake and Martin woke, I incited them to work, shifting furniture and scrubbing walls and floors, while I gathered up Feargus's personal effects and put them out on the sand for him to carry to his shack. The boys were not quite sober and lunged about rather feverishly.

Feargus grew very sober when he saw what we were doing, and once he said wistfully, "Given a free hand I could show you how to make a lovely beachcomber apartment out of those maids' rooms on the other side of the house." But I ignored this, for I really feel that he has outstayed his welcome. In paternal poses, as venerable president of the Beachcombers' Intercoastal Union (his own jest), as a neighbor — yes; but dwelling in the very heart of the house, even behaving as its host — no!

"I am accustomed to sleep in linen," he remarked, his head reproachfully on one side, on a day when I had neglected to smooth the fusty blankets of his bed. And another day he brought me his mending kit. "See that you keep it in order," he chided. And from time to time thereafter appeared ragged socks upon the basket.

Feargus, this chicanery is trivial! If you had helped us in turn, we wouldn't have put you out.

The house is cleaner, fresher. The food is all gone but a dish of apple sauce and a kettleful of lima beans. Rake is typing in the back bedroom. I can just see him around the corner.

He came walking toward me after I wrote that, and downstairs the beans boiled away and burned. So now we are going to cross the dunes and go to Wong's for dinner. I have only to put on my blue overalls, brush my hair, tie a sweater over my shoulders, and we'll start. Rake, as usual, has no preparations to make.

June 26 — Last night in Blackwall we met Martin and two young Humanists from Harvard. They wore creamy flannels and white suede shoes; their names were Maurice and Richard. Maurice is lean, with vacant eyes and a monocle. He is going to Paris next week to become a Jesuit. Richard is sturdier, but enthralled with Maurice, and never talks. With them we charged down the street, and they bought us a lavish meal while the delicate little Mr. Wong played us records of his own music.

Today, after swimming at high slack water, we lay on the sand, and suddenly I was tired out. Perhaps we have been only maudlin, after all.

Martin's voice went on, buzzing and mourning, nasal from weariness. "We alienate our love from loveliness to time . . . oh, hell, I wrote a poem about it . . . oh, Martin, shut up! . . . Who cares?"

I began to claw into the sand. "Go away!" I exclaimed. "Both of you. Go find Maurice and Richard. They're out walking, and they're such vague academic spirits they'll get lost. You told me yourself, Martin, they shut themselves into black-curtained rooms by candlelight and perfume. For Irving Babbitt's sake, rescue them from the open air of an untraditioned place!"[14]

Martin scurried off, and with a gunnysack over his shoulder Rake went north for sea clams; his listless outline against the sloping sun was all moving beauty.

Alone — quiet — quiet. Shifting into dream, I knew I was on the shore, but instead of the real ones returning, a quiet person came toward me. Philip it was, and we turned toward the sea and listened together to the incessant fall.

But I woke with the sand ground into my cheek, and my arms prickling under the twist of my body. I went up the bank into Salt House, and through the north door came Maurice and Richard, solemnly holding out before them two sticks with pink speckled crabs impaled. I thanked them, but the shells were hollow and smelled badly.

"You didn't think they were alive, did you?" I asked incredulously. They simply laughed, and their eyes slid coquettishly. I gave a farcical look at Maurice's monocle and left them to their own devices.

June 28 — It has changed. *He* is here.

We thought we would like to go fishing, and it was a way of restoring Maurice and Richard to the town. They were uneasy here, and Salt House itself was tactfully belligerent. So at twilight we trooped across the sand, and again ate our dinner at Wong's. I wore my torn overalls, a ribbon in my hair, and a sailor's woolen watch cap cocked on one side. I could see how this disturbed the two guests; they surely preferred to be seen beside well-groomed women, if at all. Later, however, when we were drinking Alexanders in Martin's room, they found I resembled Beatrice Lillie in some comic fashion, and with a tag it was all right, forgiven.

We all five sat in a row on the bed, under one high unshaded bulb of white light. We were waiting for three o'clock, when we would go to the wharves.

Martin talked of Europe as a cure for his nerves. Maurice and I commenced a footless discussion of the relative importance of critic and artist. It seemed that there was a frieze of roosters and eggs alternately arranged along the walls. According to my confused impressions, this frieze moved around rapidly, slowly, then gradually passed away. Maurice kept quoting Clive Bell, and as he became more involved, he talked French and fluttered his hands in the air.[15]

Rake and Martin were kicking their heels and making up limericks for each other.

> There was an old man from La Flynn
> Who disapproved highly of sin.
> When asked why he decried it,
> He replied, "Hell, I've tried it!"
> This ginny old man from La Flynn.

Richard sat up, listening, and staring at Maurice. He was stern and unruffled, but all of a sudden he fell over asleep. This seemed to disturb Maurice, for he stopped weaving about and passed out.

Martin flung himself across the foot of the bed, lamenting, and finally silent.

Then Rake put out the light and pulled me down beside him on the floor. I dared not submit to him, as he wished, in the crowded room with its artful unspoken emotions betwixt us all. I sat up and mixed myself another drink. Sitting at the open window, I watched the night. Summer is underway. I could hear June bugs swooping through the heavy air; now and then one of them lunged into the screen and left behind an infinitesimal vibration. Through the cotton mist shone the dull red fog light from Wood End.[16] I thought how, when I see a new thing, as now this thick after-midnight mist which swaddles the newborn season, always my first cry, with a cadence of helplessness, is: "How can I describe it?" or "How can I explain it?"

Sometimes I turned on the light, lifted Maurice's limp wrist on which he wore a watch, and wondered how I could possibly drag them all to the fishing.

When the time came, only Rake responded to my low but urgent call. Hand in hand we fumbled our way downstairs, and out into the strange world at the night's turning. Fishermen crossed the road in the distance; we knew them by their swinging lanterns. Often a blurred light shone out from a shed, and there were sudden voices and the creak of oarlocks from the water. Less than halfway through the town Rake sank down and pillowed his head on the curbstone. I, too, stretched out in the road beside him, and gave one dazed upward glance at the words *Hollyhock Cottage* before falling asleep. When the moan of a foghorn woke me later, I lay still as if I could make the instant swell, the instant of being there alone with him, before he would rise and escape me.

We reached the pier in time to follow five men down a ladder to a dory, which staggered as we dropped into it. One of them was a negro, smiling and silent. The captain, one of the men who had given us prune whiskey on The Road, appeared on the second trip out from the pier. In the tiny engine room a gong sounded, and the boat headed out to round Long Point.[17] Rake and I sat down on a board set into the cockpit of the stern. We blinked at the spray and winced grimly at the alternate rising and dipping motion.

The darkness of the harbor was thinning, the few town lights going out one by one, and behind the wharves appeared the tall dim shadow of the Monument. Near us moved the masthead lanterns of the other outgoing boats, and on the banks far to the southeast wheeled the beam of the lighthouse. When full morning came, it was foggy still and cold, with a quick drift of raindrops at intervals. The shore was nondescript, indistinct beyond the roughly graven masses of water piled up under the chisel of wind.

When we reached the first of the traps, the engine was turned off, and we drifted slowly into a pool enclosed by stakes and nets. It seemed calm at first, until one looked under the surface and saw a constant varied motion there.

The negro stood in the bow, in a hole almost waist high, armed with a boathook which he caught onto the stakes, and thus pulled us along into position. The other men stood in a row on one side of the bow, and at a signal commenced drawing in the net hand over hand, slowly, and with this motion working the boat over toward the farthest corner of the enclosure. The bowl of water in the net became more and more shallow.

The panic of the fish was frightful to see; they thrashed and leapt, and in midair gave a twist of the body in an agony that could only be exceeded by what was to follow. Into this trough the men let down a bucket with netted bottom, and scooped this along until it was full. Most of the fish were whitings, which in the water looked a dull bronze, but in the hold they were only dingy, with gray bellies.

Only once the negro spoke. When he sighted two large lobsters his eyes rolled and he danced his knees up and down in the hole. "Baby, that's mine!" It was his turn for the day's catch of lobsters.

In watching the fish, I leaned above the hold and forgot I was sleepy. Crabs sidled among the stiffening bodies and bit into them. Some of the fish died just when their mouths were gulping wide and gills spread, and I recognized in this gesticulation of anguish a motif often used in decoration. The goose fish were nightmare things, with mouths as large as their heads, and gaping throats in which lay several fish in a digestive death. These the fishermen speared aside on the deck above the hold, so that when they should clear the nets they could throw them away.

I climbed onto the top of the cabin, and Rake joined me there for a smoke. The boat rocked gently from side to side for an hour or so, while in the dory the men went from stake to stake, lifting up the net and re-tying it. They must do this every fortnight, they said, lest it never be dry and at last rot away. As Rake watched them, he smiled with a dark jealousy. I understood that he wanted something to put his hands to, exactly as these men.

One of them tied back a skate's fins and thrust it up over the cabin side at us. It looked like a shockingly white human face and had a cigarette protruding from its awful lips. Captain Hy drew a squid out from the mass of whitings and butterfish, and showed us how to prepare it for eating. "We eat them raw, when we're hungry on a trip," he said. It was without grace, long as a dinner roll, of cloudy gelatine, with crimson spots on a patch of purple coloring near the tail. My curiosity was timid.

As the fog lifted we went, under slow speed, to another trap, and went through the same procedure, only this time there were no lobsters for the negro.

"Once in a while a whale comes tearing along, and we have to cut him out of the nets."

"We don't catch so much mackerel yet, the season's late, but they'll be coming along soon now."

"Nobody knows where the mackerel goes, or the swordfish goes, in the winter."

"This was a good spring for herring, and when herring comes in, they's sure to be cod somewhere near. We got a good haul of cod this year, until a northeaster broke it up. Horse mackerel ought to be along in a couple of weeks."

They talked with pride, having things to tell us that we didn't know. I wanted to answer; their eyes, constantly on us, pled for interest, but I was more and more tired as the sun seeped through the clouds and faintly warmed the deck. I laid my head on Rake's shoulder and slept until the engines started.

About eleven o'clock we raced for the harbor, the men relaxed, with even a sort of triumph about them. In Blackwall again we dragged through the motionless blaze of noon, Rake dangling our string of cleaned and quartered fish, and drank coffee at The Spotlight. We hadn't enough money for food, but at a grocery store we charged 'gee bread and sausage, and a few other supplies.

At the house where Martin roomed, he came darting out at us. "Sh!" he warned, finger on lips. "Those two are still asleep. The landlady's going to put me out, she says, for the din and for having a woman in the room!"

We managed as far as the first hill in the woods on the Hitch, and then, sitting on a bank of last year's moss, pierced with false Solomon's seal, we tore at the bread and meat. Once we turned our heads and put our lips together, but our mouths were so weak and dusty that we only laughed and did not embrace again. I yawned and drew down some sticky sprays, late this year, from the pale stems of a shad bush. The wind went brushing along the branches, and the leaves, hung like silver brooches on the trees, turned and quivered.

It was not surprising to see Feargus crossing the railroad track and coming toward us. He waved a letter, and settled beside us to read it aloud, for letters are his career. But he had not finished when he glanced up and gave a shout.

"Ho!"

It was — Philip! He stood at the path's turning, in city clothes, quite as beautiful as ever. Even as I sprang toward him I saw Rake turn his head quickly away.

Philip dropped his pack, and for a long instant I stood inside his arms. What changes have come about that I now feared as well as longed for this?

Feargus went into Blackwall, but we three traveled the woods. Rake carried Philip's easel and the fish, while I shouldered the gunnysack of food. The heat made us dizzy.

"No," said Philip, going down the sliding sand of the long dune, "I couldn't come earlier. I think it would have been a mistake. And even once on the way I had to spend a few days with my brother Waverley."

I kept wondering why Rake had come along, and it made me realize more than ever how he never resists what is easy and near, how he gives way. On the dunes when the grass bends in complaisance to the wind it sweeps a design at the same time. Thus in still weather you will find a perfect circle lying upon the ground. I think by this same act Rake, too, has a natural design, wrought despite himself.

I walked between them and felt like a butterfly that in the intoxication of heat deliberately beats its way out over the water and, though tired, can never find the land again. I wondered which of them I really loved, and if I was a flippant woman.

As we lurched down the cutting toward Salt House, Philip ruffled up my hair from the back of the neck to the top. "They say if you scratch little dogs' heads they will love you. Do you suppose that is true?" he asked Rake.

Rake only answered "Hm-m," very sheepishly.

My heart felt clogged. It seemed as if Philip were older, more sure of himself this year, and I felt that I was going to respect him. We had parted in danger and inordinate solemn unhappiness, yet I expected, out of something newly developed, to receive the gift of quiet. I looked at his hands, mobile as a face, the nails fanwise, and the fingers wide at the ends to feel as much as possible. I put, perhaps, more trust in those hands than in the face, which is usually shut. . . . Also I wondered if there could be any trouble between these two, and I thought, "No; each of them is wrapped in pride."

When we reach the house Rake fell upon Feargus's old bed in the boiling room. One can depend on his sleeping, no matter what the crisis, I thought almost resentfully.

Philip sat down in the storage room, and I sat on the floor in front of him. First he smiled down, then he laughed and pounced upon me. "Just as I remembered, but I couldn't be sure," he said. "The same hair growing in points, and little ears, and — " I lifted my face so his fingers could run lightly over it in the old skillful way, as if he were blind and could only know it by touch.

"You have nice legs, too!" and suddenly he buried his head in my arms in confusion. I could feel that he was as timid as I. Who knows? Perhaps Rake's presence in the house — silent, but thus all the more oppressive — composed a design more literal than he would admit aloud, less accidental beneath the chancy winds than I believed.

"How childish I am," Philip whispered; "but it is good to be here. Do you know, I almost dared not to come!"

I held my breath.

"Why?"

He would not answer but lifted me to my feet, and we went upstairs. After getting into my bathing suit, I watched him unpack his few things: old shirts, trousers, paints, brushes and pencils, a book or two, singularly all these in his own colors — old black, chartreuse, dusky green, mostly the colors of shabbiness. His face had kept its quiet luster. Something certain grew in me as I watched, and my thoughts referred less often to the boy downstairs.

The sea was without horizons, one with the blank paper-white sky. After the relief of swimming, Philip walked down the shore, and I fell asleep in the same sandy niche as the day before and dreamed the same dream, that Philip had come to me at last. But as I dreamed, I seemed awake and saying, "It is only something I'm dreaming. I mustn't believe it." Then slowly, slowly returned the knowing. Still in the utmost fatigue (last night's revels now far), I dragged up into the sea chamber and fell upon my bed. Soon Philip returned and came back up the stairs.

When it was fully dark we rose, and wakened Rake for supper. I'm sure it was one of the happiest moments in years — private to me, and never to be disturbed — to see Philip there by the table. Feargus did not appear, I don't know why. Working together we cooked the fish, dressed tomatoes, and baked cornbread.

"What's it like down in Mexico?" asked Rake.

"I can't really say. I do know I don't like their system on the border. They took away all the drawings I made in Mexican bars and arrested me for staying late over the line one night."

He told the full story haltingly, in the tone I remember, through which drifts mingled disgust and resignation. He had spent ten days on a rock pile, having no money to pay his fine, but he seemed not to wish to talk of this. I understood that he had repudiated the experience. Rake listened and often laughed.

"'How'd you like San Quentin, fella?' they asked me, 'and Joliet' and a lot of other prisons. They talked about them the way traveling men talk about hotels. I couldn't go back on them, could I? All I could answer was 'Fine!' or 'Rotten!' and they weren't satisfied, but even rather suspicious."

This braced Rake; this was in his own rowdy line. I had no illusions, however, about the chance of their liking each other.

The day went out without the least allure. It simply disappeared.

Rake left Salt House after supper. "So long. See you sometime," he blurted, and hurried out. I wonder if his simplicity is going to rescue him. He is unique, and there's no telling, but I don't believe in that simplicity.

I went to the top of the companionway and sat in the dark, twining my fingers in the fishnet that hung about the railing. I really wish him not to be hurt, but I could not have let him go before. I came here to Salt House with the thoughtful intention of living directly and truthfully. All that has happened could have happened in no other way. I pondered no further than this when Philip came up the stairs.

He sat a step below me. We said nothing, so it was as if we had told each other everything. It was the peace and rest for which I have been longing, rest more exquisite perhaps than we shall ever know together again.

I have to report that later this was all broken up by the midnight arrival of Martin, Maurice, and Richard. We were asleep when there were scratching treads outside, and then preposterous cries of "Champagne! Champagne! Champagne!" My first thought flew to Rake. Where had he gone, then, if not to them? Was he in the camp, rolled in moldy blankets on the ground, hearing the false tiptoeing wind?

Martin, who has perhaps never heard of Philip, treated him candidly as an apparition. The lamp in the storage room cast a dismal cone of less than darkness upon the wall, and touched no faces. I prattled, but Philip, poised on a wicker stool and wearing a ragged crimson robe, was attractive and troublous to the Humanists, and they soon took their leave.

I blamed no one, but knew they had planned to accept my risqué hospitality. Martin dropped upon the blue divan, and today he is still here.

I rose early and slipped about the kitchen in the ruddy first light. I am drinking coffee at the table and writing in this journal. Through the doorway I can see Martin's elfish head cushioned on his arms. Thought of the past days of this month clamors in me to defend my comrades against Philip's stare. But he is here, and a new day is beginning.

I hear the tide slashing, and gulls whimpering with greed.

Later — Feargus came in this afternoon. I was alone in the storage room, resting in a long chair. He was just from town, where he had picked up numerous cocktails. I think he had stopped at the gin tree, too, for he was flushed.

"As to prohibition," he announced, "*die ganze Welt* has gone berserker."

I put down my book and listened to his generalizations for some time. "But I see what's on your mind," he said at last. "Philip in town?"

I nodded.

"He has a lovely manner," he went on, cocking his head over on one side.

"Feargus," I said, "what shall I do? You know the way I feel about both of them. When I'm dispassionate it doesn't seem right, but I can't seem to find any real distress in it. If I lived in a town I might insist on trouble, don't you suppose?"

"Here," he said slowly, "everything smooths over; even a storm only leaves the sand clean-swept."

"And erases the footprints."

We both smiled, but I went on, "That's what I distrust. There *must* be danger somewhere."

"Surest thing, Little Mischief, there is. It is very fine to live true to yourself, but mark my words — if you can't choose between them you will finally lose them both."

"Oh!" I sat upright in dismay. "Do you think so? Oh, no!" It made me feel hollow, as if I hadn't eaten for days, the very thought!

"And then," said Feargus, leaning backward and sticking his thumbs in his armpits. "I shall be the Ultimate and Enduring Lover."

"Good old Feargus," I said, with a touch of cruelty, to which his malice instantly responded. "By the way, Martin's in love with you, too," he said warily. "He told me all about it the afternoon you took your Rake upshore. It must be a great satisfaction to you to have us all running in the circle around you."

"Feargus! Isn't there excitement enough for you now, without pulling poor Martin into it, too? He's my friend, and I haven't tried a single inch to make him anything else. You leave him out!"

He kissed my hand and went away. I went out on the dune to my watching place. From the hollow below I heard the flickering voices of crickets. Philip, you are too long away.

There is a belting of woods below this dune, hardly more than a thicket. The path going through deepens and widens almost to a pool. There is a story that when Salt House was flourishing, a span of horses sank under this path. Dwarf oaks and alder grow alongside, and seeded grasses grow lushly up through the water.

I stroke the down on my arms and scrape up little patterns on the sand. Now and then there's the hot swing of a fly. I try not to brood on those words: *"If you can't choose between them you will finally lose them both."* No! I'll think of something else. Philip, when you return we will eat our fish and fruit, and strange light bread, this time in the boiling room, which today I cleared and washed. There the windows are high above the lockers on one side, and along the other side is a shelf. The table stands down the center on a thick straw mat, built like a high bench, and I've restored to it the single white dish of fruit. These — windows, table, shelf — make three long lines in the narrow room. White walls and ceiling. Hardly anything else: A few colored pottery bowls and plates on the shelf, and in the farther corner a cabinet of shells and old fishbones. Once the whole end of this room used to be thrown open to the winter air after the bitter water was boiled, but now it is firmly walled in. Our jackets hang beside the pantry door on rusty hooks.

Philip said this morning, after I had given hours to the room, "Come now, Judith; I don't like you in this vigorous mood. It's too like my mother."

"Well, that's who I'm supposed to be like, you know," and I was unrepentant.

Now that I think of it, how little we really say to each other, how seldom we talk. Philip, you do not like the way I let myself go — scrubbing here in the boiling room today, and my madly festive dinners with Rake, Martin, and the Humanists. I can see that you think when I do such things I remove vigor and exuberance from my work. But I shall tell you that I have to resolve these excitements into something I can understand. I have come to a time for living.

There you are! I see you descending the path. I know from afar, because of the way you walk, your knees sagging and the legs thrown out — dangling, from the hips. I recognize you by your sack, too, and a canvas under your arm. A long shambling shadow is at your side in the late whiskey-colored light.

I will dig a hole in the sand for this notebook, and then I will run down the path, through the woods, and meet you. You will close me into your arms, and we will smile back and forth, but I am afraid we will not have much to talk about. Last night the silence enthralled me, but now . . .

Watch out, Philip, lest in shying the commonplace you'll miss all reality. I think the actual forms of life cannot be scorned, and I think that your smile sometimes hardens to a grin, your sensibility, through overmuch cherishing, is no more vitally precious than virginity. Now — I must hurry.

June 30 — Yes, we ate in the boiling room as I planned. Everything stood out with sharp edges. The glossed Canton plates and the flat blue of the floor harmonized with that other blue — the squares of night in the windows beyond the lamp.

I was wrong about our ways together, for Philip talked. He told of a place where he stopped in New Mexico. "The room had four hollow tile walls, white-washed, with a grease mark here and there to satisfy the esthete. The stove now and then demanded more coal from the bucket, in return for which an aroma of heat rather than heat itself penetrated the emptiness bounded and held in by the hollow walls. There was also an iron bed, painted brilliant yellow presumably to add the 'cozy' touch. To the left, occupying at least half of the garage (and well it might), was my beloved Buick truck, piled high with tow rope, oil cloth, and parcels of various shapes tied in brown and green paper with frayed hemp around their bellies.

"There I sat, with my nose pointed west. Why? Remaining the absurd optimist. Outside, the moon was the same that lends itself to the cosmic quality of the dunes; there it illuminated a dusty street cluttered with dry goods stores, and hay and grain emporiums.

"The camaraderie of the road there! When one opened one's door on the way to the 'sanitary' toilet, five doors opened simultaneously, five boudoir heads stuck out like grotesque masks dangling on broomsticks.

"I was looking for the faint purple and blue mountains, and I tried not to come back here, for I wanted to stand clear, to have no one, not even you, lay hands on my life."

"I can understand," I said in a low voice, yet it wasn't really true. I didn't understand, for when he laid hands on *my* life, he brought me away clear from all else.

"But I was too weak," he continued. "I couldn't stay away."

"You ought rather to say, in courtesy, that the feeling was too strong."

He bowed his head but gave me a long look from under his eyebrows.

"Yes!" he whispered.

Suddenly my dismay gave way before a recollection of spring. "So that night when you telephoned from Toledo, when your voice came over half the country saying, 'I *do* love you!' you had only just then decided?"

"Yes."

I swiftly wondered if I should say, "But now our hours here these last two years, pledges and wishes and all, my thinking I had this one thing as surely as morning and night — all these are denied."

I didn't say anything like that. I sat remembering how after that telephone call I had gone careering around a block of the town where I lived, passing the open doors and windows of the lighted houses, passing the blaring radio sounds, and outside them all I was jigging my feet and pressing my clasping arms tight — antics performed in what seemed then a reasonable joy.

I realized now for the first time what a fragile vessel I am holding, after all. I will have to be careful lest it crack or break.

I poured the coffee and took my cup to the lockers, where I arranged myself knowingly like a decoration against the bright wall. Spying through half-closed eyes I continued to see, almost with pleasure, how easily this young man and his affection for me can be smashed.

The next day, returning from Blackwall, I saw Feargus emerge from his shack, then Philip, and a minute or two later, Rake. They had been there all afternoon, shooting out over the shore and then helping Feargus put down some beer. We all walked on to Salt House together. That night we talked a great deal about Russia, and then I demanded "Philip! please, more of your travels."

"As you will," he said. "Shall I tell you about Santa Fe, for instance? It was rather like Spain, except that scrub and timber covered the mountains, with a red cone sometimes protruding from the sea of dark green. When I wanted to paint them, snow fell. I had to go south and into Arizona, still looking for the mountains I wanted — stark, with cactus, dead sky unbroken by clouds."

"What were the people like out there?"

"I saw only other wayfarers — red-faced men with eyeglasses, and thin little women pressing their knees together for shame of their khaki knickers. When the men asked, 'And how are the roads through Texas?' I used to want to curse them, because they were such ugly people; saying something like, 'May your children be born free of hangnails, but with a tourist camp for a manger.'"

When he stopped talking Rake only said, "Hm-m!" in comment, and then, "Have an apple, Feargus, do."

Feargus began a speech, though he was befuddled. His ideas as well as gestures were expansive, and he ended with the statement, "As for me, I'm going to found a new school of social and literary criticism through the pages of the Blackwall *Hour*."

We looked at one another aghast. Had Feargus's mind slipped a few cogs? Philip went in by the fireplace, and out from the darkness swayed the music of his accordion. Feargus took Rake firmly by the arm and they floundered out.

Cold in my bare feet, I moved the lamp to the pantry and cleared up the dishes as swiftly as possible. Philip joined me, and when the work was done we blew out the lamp and, hand in hand, felt our way along the wall to go upstairs. All night the water fell upon the shore with its indescribable sound of something brittle that is breaking softly.

July 1 — Feargus is coming from town with alcohol as a gift from Rake, also with four quarts of ginger ale. Question is, will he weather the gin tree?

I am lying in a long chair dragged out to the headland above the kitchen windows. Rake is on his way to New York again, Martin in the house somewhere, Philip gone over the Hitch for cigarettes.

The day declines, and the evening wind blows softly.

Later — We climbed, Philip and I, out on the ridge pole to see the moonrise. As it went higher its path was broken up, and in ripples quite unexpectedly we saw a golden slapstick comedy of falling saucers. A whole pile of them stacked up noiselessly, then by twos and threes dropped down while other plates magically filled up the game.

July 2 — Philip went again to Blackwall today. He has found some friends, whose names, he tells me, are Loyal and Ione.

I am in bed in the sea chamber, waiting for him. The warm lamplight on the walls is like new paint.

Have I, in my notebook, I wonder, made the relationships among these people of Salt House mobile in all senses, mobile even beyond the cinema way? Also I wonder if I can express my point of view in letting these relationships develop as they do. If, by touching the poverty grass on the dunes with my fingertips, and the beach plum bushes and the dusty miller plants, or by biting into the flavor of checkerberry leaves in the woods, I know that each thing has form and *is*, I can as well trust what happens between these even more animate beings.

Good! I am working out; I am becoming a girl who begins to know.

July 3 — Philip appeared in the middle of the night, and, lying back on the darkness, we talked. The windows blued, and the darkness going away left us asleep.

Today Philip paces the floor, getting ready to paint. The picture, for which I shall sit, will be one who, barelegged and in a yellow tennis dress, leans forward between white walls. A white framed mirror holds another space wherein appear again her shoulder and arm. Over the flesh will flow green-blue daylight.

He does not understand words, and they come out of his mouth mostly half incoherent. This offends me, not personally, but in that it makes all wording untrustworthy. If he does not savor words, how can he have toward books the clean critical bite? And is it proof of disarray or hesitations in thought and feeling?

What is this? I am not beginning to suspect him, am I? Sometimes I remember that his brother has the same gestures and even the same low and significant fainting voice. Are the gestures, the voice, the brother's distinctions, not Philip's own, then? And I see in vivid print that figure in the flannel dressing gown, in whom a narrow spirit lives without activity. Two brothers cannot — must not — be alike. It frightens me.

July 4 — In the sea chamber.

I learn my lessons.

Four came last night: Loyal, Ione, Maurine, and Willy. All one can say of Loyal is that he is a laughing boy, and of Ione there is more to say, yet when all is seen, he is without effort all that Ione apes. She is small, with puffy thighs, a swollen face with clever sleepy eyes, and flat neglected hair. Does she arouse others with the way her mask breaks up into side glances and into a smile that is a flashing distortion? Is she simply candid, or is she steadfast in a pose? Sooner or later, at any rate, the Blackwall people have all talked about her. After you come to like her you feel that she is sucking in your liking.

The other girl, Maurine, is quite another kind of creature and has more savor. She lives in Willy's cold white house as in his body, and only comes alert when she is reminded there have been other women there before her, and may come after. She is long and thin, with high wide eyes and a tremendous mouth. I've known her for two seasons. She does cartoons and has a morose satirical manner — a thorough sophisticate who doesn't bother about smartness. Arty girls, both, wearing men's shirts and trousers. Maurine's meager life is a natural attainment; she works too hard to consider its appearance, but I wouldn't put it above Ione to have cabbage smells in the air of her attic purposely as the symbol of a struggling career. Loyal hasn't detected her pose; her sublime incoherence, coupled with the pseudo-significance of her smile, has put him off completely. He grins at her occasional outbursts of, "Shut yer face, yer dumb cluck!" always in surprising relief against her fine silences.

As for Willy, he is uncommonly lean, his fine dirty yellow hair falling limply from a withdrawn forehead to the back of his head. His eyes are pale, his lips colorless, yet regardless of this remote effect, or perhaps because of it, he possesses a kind of vague distinction and prides himself upon it. Maurine's desire is sufficient reason for him to accept her; I'm sure any desire *he* ever feels is a lackluster thing.

Always poor, they are, all of them, always just touched with colds, and endure a constant though slight bronchitis as well as cigarette coughs.

Now I will write it: Philip's arms were around Ione, and he was kissing her. This is the first time in my life I have been hurt this way, and it points me into age — age which one never forgets is followed by death. I dare not think, dare not think. I knew it without the words for it, even before I saw it, when he came upstairs; his face against mine burned unnaturally, and he questioned in haste, "Have you gotten a slant on Ione? She's swell!" I suppose that is why I left my typing and went softly down into the pantry and saw them.

I came right back here again, and drew this notebook to me.

I must not be angry, I must not. There's Rake. I will keep this hurt though, for even this is something between us, something passing from him to me. Oh, Christ!

I think I like Ione, and certainly I can't blame another girl for feeling what I feel. Oh, dear, there *is* a pride that's hurt. For how can I go down there to eat with them, how can I?

Loyal and Feargus are chortling together on the blue divan, and the others walking on the shore below, while Ione and Philip prepare a dinner. This would, they planned, enable me to finish my article for the mail.

I *will* go down there when they call me. I shall be an actress at the dinner table. I thought the time for that was all over, with my past life, but the necessity commences again.

Why did he have to do this so *soon*? I have given up Rake, haven't I? He has gone to New York, hasn't he?

Philip may have Ione, if he wants, without question of me. I'll not let it matter in the long run, only now.

That he came upstairs and kissed me — wasn't *nice*.

I can endure this strange sensation. I love him so much, I have so much faith in our love — or have I? Insidiously I again recall Waverley's identical mannerisms. Are Philip's ways only mannerisms, too?

I'd like hysteria, since it's a rapid purge, but no — only when Ione leaves, I'll sleep alone.

I must not forget life is not a straight line, but changes, goes on differently.

There! I did go down there just now. I *can* do it. I caught a moth, turned it over, and showed them its intent little owl's face. They paid it perfunctory attention. Philip tipped up Ione's chin. "*Your* face is something like a clock," he said, and it is true that its lozenge shape is blank and inexpressive.

I think less of you, Philip — that's all it will mean to us. I'm sure I am right, that I think less of you, but that we can go on with our life together.

This afternoon, in Blackwall, I saw that she would go after him. She was walking with Loyal, and we came up behind them. Without turning she said, "Hello, Philip, yer dumb cluck. Yer goddammed fool, don't spill this clam bucket." I knew that she had seen me, wished to impress me with the familiarity betwixt them; this because she feared me, and *this*, in turn, because she badly wanted him. Easily, I thought, as bubbles, do our emotions, the emotions of women, from profundity well up to the surface.

They have started drinking.

I am disgusted with him — with his kiss at the top of the stairs; why did he do that? He should not have done that. I repeat myself because my thoughts repeat as I drum my fists on my forehead.

I shall set myself to watch now, to see if there is a falseness about him, after all. *Sincere* has just come to be a lovely word to me.

Later — At dinner, in the boiling-room, I tried not to see how many times they found it necessary to go into the kitchen together. And I thought bitterly how simple the meal was after the long preparation. I said, "I always like to smash things," and dashed an old bottle from the cabinet against the wall until it broke, and the pieces spurted in all directions. Philip ran out of the room and looked askance around the edge of the door. He and Feargus, who was twinkling and nodding, alone could tell that I was not gay. And, of course, Ione looked a bit nervous.

Then I said, "I don't feel like sleep tonight. I'm going to Blackwall with the rest of you. There's a night club opening — a party at The Schooner. Who else wants to come?"

Philip drew his eyelids and upper lip down, with the exposed expression both he and Waverley assume before the mirror, more particularly in his case a weary, bizarre mask without any revelations. Then he turned on his heel, apparently his feeling too attenuated, his lips too weak, to form a reply. But we are going — and whatever happens I'll write it down tomorrow.

July 5 — This morning nothing moved but the water at the edge of the sea. The waves were rolling up great liquid foaming masses which fell with a heavy sound, and which, by a curious action of the wind, were drawn back in convulsions upon themselves. The horizon of the sand dunes lay quietly in space; there was not the slightest vibration of heat or light anywhere, and all was dim and still before the coming rain.

We went to the party last night, the first one of the season, and were too miserable to realize these pastels. Salt House lay waiting for us like a loyal animal.

In this motionless forenoon we lay flat on the divan, and Philip was gently manipulating his wrists above him in the air. Because the alcohol had been so cheap and bad we found our eyesight focusing improperly, and our hearts were rank and heavy. We knew that whereas simplicity lay about us here, artless as water, our hands were now too fragile to reach into it. The clock had stopped, leaving a hollow where we were accustomed to its thick and steady beat.

I lay on my back, legs crossed in the air, mouthing a cigarette, and after a while felt strong enough to talk.

"Like the party?"

"Not very. I battled for you," Philip reminded me.

I pressed my lips scornfully between the phrases of my responses. "Didn't you though! But weren't nearly as disgusting as Willy. He kept bleating."

"Why did Feargus and Willy have to follow us and find us sitting down in the road?"

"We looked so incompetent, that's why they followed us," I replied. "I wasn't so helpless, but you pulled me down again. Finally when we did go along the Hitch you were chanting 'Over the hills to the poorhouse,' and Feargus was snapping the whip with us and bashing our heads together, and we all kept tumbling down in a heap."

If the party had only had a joyous significance, if the music had been good, if we could have become excited or seen our new life opening up before us — but there had been only people continually walking back and forth, watching each other like cats or celebrities. We all sat at one table. Today, out of the party's superfluity of words and its forced, driven experiences, we needed to be tired and speechless. We recalled our friends as having yesterday been stimulating, chosen people, but in the drab remembered light of the past evening they were unspeakably dull figures. Willy recited dirty verses and boasted to us afterward, "When a small-town crowd wants big-time stuff I'll give it to them." And he kept leaning over me whispering, "You're swell — you're a *type* like me." He pronounced it to rhyme with weep.

Now it was over, we felt left alone, and even ourselves no longer either diverting or worthy. If time was passing we could not feel it, and we were both removed from what had once been real. When my feeble pulse began to revive — I had been putting my finger on it from time to time — I lifted my arms in the air. They were trembling at the elbows. With that gesture I could either strike or implore. I glanced warily at Philip. "Two spiders in one web," I mused idly, wanting thin words. He lay still, but with his eyes open and doggedly intent upon the ceiling. The fragments of a blue glass Bromo-Seltzer bottle were scattered on the floor at his feet. And then I turned away and closed my eyes, for my heart had seemed to contract and to shut all its valves with alarm. If Phillip felt distaste for me, if he would not take me in . . .

I inhaled with a sound that fairly sobbed on the air. And the hand that had closed itself upon my heart now loosened and released so sudden a flow of blood that my arms fell at my sides, throbbing and more helpless than before. If the clock would start, if time would begin, and events move upon us — but we were only being left in a hollow place out of time, dropped and left there insecurely.

The party was a false thing, and here the flowing sea was almost upon us, and the bad alcohol still in our veins, and we in a long-inactive room where weakness pinned us down.

At length, with an effort Philip spoke. "Someone is coming." For a few moments we seemed to feel a gravitational pull toward us from a distance. And later we were not surprised to hear a knock at the door. I looked again at Philip, who was weaving his fingers in the most abandoned idleness I've ever seen. He continued his meaningless gaze at the ceiling, but his eyebrows managed to rise with an expression of inquiry. Ah, I thought, you are neither proud nor sorry; you are quite simply mine, and you know it. You can't be troubled with Ione, and so it's all over with her, and you lie here in the inertia of a hangover. Your emotion last night was untimely, but now —

The knock came at us again.

My thought was as slow as my pulse and shaped itself no faster than speech. But now the unpronounced words continued in my waiting mind, and with all the egoistic intensity of my desire: you prefer the timeless certainty of me.

And indeed, Philip had turned on his side and was looking at me ardently. I felt racily myself again as I rose and put my hand on the doorknob, but then hesitated, and called out with an expression of confusion and surprise, "Perhaps you'd better not — perhaps you'd *rather* not come in. You see — we have no time here."

Ione's voice, from the other side of the door, had an insinuating bravado. "Is Philip here? I came to see Philip."

I gave all myself to Philip as I looked at him, at the same time mutely conveying his opportunity should he choose it. Then my eyes blunted on his figure, so white and unheld at that moment it might have been shaped out of the circumfluent air. And he, in return, I know, saw that I would be ruthless toward him always.

"Tell her," he murmured, "we're temporarily 'out.' You needn't explain eternity."

I repeated the message, dazzled. Ione was quiet a while, then suddenly she shouted at us, "To hell with it!" Shortly after, Philip rose, took my arm, and together we opened the door to where footprints led away over the bank of sand, footprints which by now are rubbed out in the night's rain.

"You're a strange kind of a girl," he said caressingly.

"Shut your face, yer dumb cluck!" I said, triumphantly mocking him, the footprints, the party, the hangover.

Under the moist freshening strength of the evening wind seiners and mackerel boats were coming in, rounding the Race.[18] The sun rayed out and pierced through the clouds with a single live cinder. Close to us, the long blades of beach grass beat about in their best lightly fencing way and glittered in the sudden light.

We stood in the doorway, looking over the profound flood of the sea, and behind us in the house, with the vibrations of recovery, the pendulum of the clock commenced again to swing.

July 8 — A few days ago a flock of tourists walked right into Salt House, without knocking, and stood staring in the middle of the storage room. "Quite a ruin, quite a ruin!" a lean man with a camera and a beret repeated. Philip rose up from where he was reading Margaret Anderson and Gorky, turn and turn about, on the blue divan.[19] "This is a private residence," he said, with frigid shyness. They scattered, but the embarrassment was all on our side.

Another day a couple walked in and saw him trying to build up some clay from the shingle downshore around an armature. "Oh, Freddy, look at the stature!" the woman said. Philip tore the clay off the figure and flung it with a splash to the floor.

We painted a sign after that: *Salt House — 50 cents admission fee.* And since we've put it outside, the tourists keep their distance.

We moved today into a shed beside the barn, for other people have rented Salt House.

Tonight, when the ship lantern was lit and hanging on the wall, we heard lurching voices. And here I must explain that in the past few days a group of uncouth silent youths, led by Rake, have sprawled in the shack.

"*You* must discard these meaningless people, for it's your fault they're here," Philip told me with a soft ferocity.

Feargus, who was having a cup of tea and alcohol, leaned back with a watching tolerant smile. We waited, and for a while the sea's rhythm was undisturbed. Then the boys appeared at the dorm looking a trifle silly, hopeful silly, with queer hats and a banner of leaves tied to a long stick. I treated them with disparaging quietude as they came into the shadows of the place. They ranged themselves on the bed. Suddenly Philip, who was stirring soup for our meal, roared at them, "Have you no sensitivity?" and bolted through the door.

"Well!" I breathed, adding to myself that sensitivity is something one doesn't talk about, my dear one.

Rake also went out, and plunging along with obvious discontent, dropped down over the bank. In the windless drizzling twilight, I talked to him about not giving himself to such worthless boys, and not intruding them on his elders. When I finished, I squatted down on my heels and hung my head. With long spaces between his words he replied, "But I can't hurt people . . . You wouldn't kick a dog — why do you want me to kick a man? . . . If I hurt them they might never forget it as long as they live . . . and I shouldn't forget it, either, as long as that . . . Jesus Christ, after all! I've had them five days; you've had them only a few hours . . . And I have to entertain them! They followed me up here from New York. Their car is being repaired, and they can't pay the bill . . . I've got to wait until my next allowance comes before I can pay it . . . That's why I'm drunk all the time — it's such a goddamned bore."

"Do you think me a bitch?" As I asked this my hands and knees were shaking, whether from the chill, or emotion, I couldn't tell.

"No, I think you're quite swell."

I wondered if he was keeping me from hurt also. I hunted down the feeling in his face, and he looked bewildered. Rake — I know how it is with him. He wants the absolute of things so terribly that he distrusts every outside value and himself as well. Out of this naive distress, overlaid with animal spirits, he is, in Blackwall, shaping himself a mythological form.

He roused, saying, "Well, I'll take them back to town." Soon I saw them all come filing out of the shed and go shambling up through the cutting. They *did* look like a helpless flock of something or other — rather like goats than sheep.

Oh, Philip, where was the harm? Your disdain is born of your weakness.

July 9 — I have posed all day. The picture comes along. An hour ago a thunderstorm came burgeoning over the water, and we rushed into Salt House to close the windows, for the tenants were in town. We lingered a while in the harsh white stormlight of the kitchen, playing records and jigging about like puppets.

I am writing this, and Feargus has just appeared. I boast of Philip's daylong work, to which he adds with rue, "And me out wenchin'!" Between his knees stands an umbrella, for he borrowed one in Blackwall and crossed the dune with it braced above his tumbled head.

He further declares that he is tired from town, that he is "off that world and all its minions."

This life goes on, close and warm between the whitewashed walls of the shed, but it is soon to end.

July 10 — Yes, soon to end. The new family in Salt House are going to need the shed for their guests, and they have offered us the use of their apartment in New York. They are going to use my little horse, Jezebel. When I carried this news to Philip, he said in his softest voice, "The time is ripe for a metropolitan summer."

July 11 — As evening came on, a dry windy tempest swept along, close to the ground. We were walking back from the shingle, that barren place between the beach and the shore, paved with loose stones. Suddenly the colors of our clothes came out vividly as new fabric, and we ourselves stood out like two poster figures glued against the gray bulging screen of sky. Bundles of seaweed ran as if they had legs, all in one direction, and fast-driven spatting grains of sand struck our faces. The wind was darkly scratching the water like a rowdy old woman with dirty fingernails on a windowpane. Yet all this while the southwestern sky, Jupiter's province, was calm as a sheet. Two crows flew over, strayed from inland, and crying their dismay at sight of the sea. Far out, viper lightning licked and stung the water's farthest edges.

Then it turned dark, and we ran out of the wildness without escaping the lonely catastrophe of storm. Afterward the night was dark and sultry. We put the lamp on a chair by the bed and lay naked, our limbs entangled, reading. Before we knew he was there, or could cover ourselves, Rake came in and stood swaying, with bloodshot eyes, rumpling his hair. He looked as if he hadn't slept in twenty nights.

The three of us pretended that we were not disconcerted. "I came to bottle the beer that's in the barn," he said. "May I borrow your lantern?" I nodded, and he unhooked it from the wall.

"I'm going to New York again on Monday," he went on. "And as I bought a motorcycle, I could take you both with me. It hasn't an extra seat, but you might manage to sit on. Save you carfare, anyway."

"That would be fine!" I exclaimed, and I really was excited. Philip said, "I think I will go by the boat, but you had better go this way if it pleases you."

"Monday, then. I'll come out early and help carry your stuff." He went clumsily, and we blew out the light. We lay on the far sides of the bed, and the moon rose through the windows, split across like any fruit.

July 12 — I am a little angry with Philip. I give up my day to the picture, yet he doesn't quite feel like working yet and reads instead. I cannot, in the meantime, plunge into my own work, so I have to just putter about, reading, nibbling, getting nowhere. I suppose he is disturbed about Rake and the beer-making that has been going on in the barn. I'll have my own good friends make beer if they like.

That's all right; it will work itself out, but what really annoys me is that when I wish to sit for him he only reads. I feel sure that we have become, both of us, too studiously subtle about our relationship. It is true that we are both distinctively acute, so acute as to be almost crafty.

Now — I guess he is going to work. I watch without speaking. I love him again! And I am only a bad girl.

July 14 — Rescued! from what has become overclose and overwarm.

It came about this way. Sometimes one becomes restless as a bird. At such times, in response to whatever gesture I may throw on the air, something new happens to me. Yesterday morning I said, "No, I can't pose today; it is so near the end of our time here." Philip was content to rest also. The sky was pale with heat, but when we ran out into the water we found it to be very cold. On the bars, half a mile out, was tossing something that looked like a raft. Philip swam out for it and returned, pushing it before him, with the current driving him aside. As I waited I looked over my shoulder toward Feargus's shack, and there saw Rake standing on the platform by the door, yawning and stretching in the morning sunlight. I called, and he came galloping toward us, and helped to pull the raft in through the breakers.

When Philip went home to warm himself, I climbed up to the shack with Rake. The Interpreter was trying to drive him away, and save his beer.

"Go 'way!" he kept saying to me, as I sat idly on the step, digging my toes into the sand. "S'long as you're here, *he* won't go."

"Do you really think so? Is that true?" I asked, looking anxiously up into Feargus's face. I needn't have asked. Already I knew; I had seen it the night before, when Rake came for the lantern. There was, in his look, still the feeling he once had.

Rake came out of the shack and solemnly handed me a bucket of salted crabs, which I carried down onto the beach where I cracked and ate them. I sat for a long time. No boats were in sight but a single freighter, burying its nose in white water and rising exuberantly and gracefully. There were Sunday people looming on various stretches of the shore, and I thought, "I'll ask the first one who passes near to eat these with me."

The first one was a browned and chubby man in all white, who amiably stopped when I held out the bucket and queried, "Have some?" Rake came, half falling down the bank, and together we shaped the figure of an Egyptian woman lying flat on the moist sand. The man's name was William, and he invited us to a party. We said we would go.

Later in the day I meant to explain to Philip why I wanted to go, but I couldn't express what I felt, because of his sullen withdrawing eyes. He does not question what I do, yet even in marriage I did not feel more restraint. I will try to put down here what I couldn't say.

It is this, that on any one occasion I might say, "No, this is not valuable, and I will not waste part of my scant total here." But then how would the total be made up? I would not have, afterward, for the occasion, the slightest degree of wit or even a particle of criticism. It is best to determine, once and for all, *I will go.*

But I didn't say any of this. I perfumed my ears and mouth and throat, brushed out my hair, and just before sunset hurried into Blackwall. All the people in the house to which we were asked were going to The Showboat, a remodeled four-master out of Bath, painted with mermaids and clowns, fastened to the town pier. I told them I would wait for Rake, and we would join them later.

Standing behind the curtains and looking out, everything on the street seemed to be warming and expanding. Perhaps the drink in my hand accounted for this effect; it was made of distilled alcohol, and clean and bitter as green buds. (These were my last sober moments until the next day, when I found myself wandering over the dunes in a dry early sunlight.)

Mischievously Rake had hidden himself in the barn at Salt House, drinking some sour unbottled beer, but at last he, too, came over the Hitch and down the street.

"I'll have to go to Amanda's and borrow a clean shirt of her husband," he explained. "Will you go, too?"

We faced each other, smiling, left behind the others in a room so different from the peculiar barren disorder of Salt House that it seemed opulent, smug, and foreign.

"I can't get over you," he said. "I've tried, but I can't. Every twenty minutes I remember you. Even in hell I would remember you."

I tried to pull his words into me greedily, and that singular feeling of expansion continued. Almost I said aloud, "Then why didn't you speak for me? Why didn't you ask for me? Why don't you make any effort?"

But I couldn't say a pressing, dramatic thing like that.

We took a cushion from the couch, and with it I mounted the back fender of the motorcycle. My cape flew behind in the wind, as we rode to Dangerfield, and it fell in its folds again as Rake pushed slowly in under the dark still bank of trees and hills where Amanda and her husband live. He changed into a clean shirt but went on wearing his duck trousers, which were immoderately soiled with grease and dust. I was surprised that he changed at all, for he prefers to look like someone who has thrown himself upon a current with no idea of touching any shore again.

It was full darkness when we descended the last hill into Blackwall. This night my feeling about Rake was on the point of some sort of explosive flowering, resolving into a form more recognizable than ever.

As we passed the house of our host we flung the cushion behind the hedge. Rake is idle the instant he is off the motorcycle, and so we walked along the pier and over the gangplank of The Showboat with flagrant nonchalance.

"I don't like people in their thirties," he confided when we had found seats with our party. "They become complacent, with a sort of overripe wit."

"Quick, then!" I said. "Let's make faces at them!" We turned our heads toward people at other tables and made the worst faces we knew, and then we rose and offered our boxes of popcorn to strangers, with sober elaborate courtesy.

The host stood by my chair and asked me to dance, just to restrain these antics, I knew. He seemed to be acting in blind politeness, and on the verge of rushing away to be polite in some other place. I was quite embarrassed, and still more so when he said, with a duck of his head, "It's a good floor, isn't it?"

I looked at the floor. "Yes," I answered helplessly, "isn't it." Over my shoulder I saw Rake escaping behind the orchestra to the foredeck outside. When the music ended I slipped out the door. Rake was eighty feet up, almost at the top of the mast, and he was looking down at the water overlaid with the moonlight in a separate quivering stream. Then someone came out of a cabin that had been changed into an office, and called up the ladder, "Come down out of there! We're nursing a guy now that fell down from there last week. We're not going to be responsible if *you* fall." When Rake reached the deck he said, "Falling off there would be a swell way of dying. Provided you went into the water and didn't hit the deck instead."

As we danced, the bottom of my box of popcorn broke open, and all the white grains spread into a garden over the floor. "Let's go away," Rake suggested. "The management is getting cross with us, anyway."

We went back into the Breakwater End and went to another party.[20] Soon all of our group arrived there, too. The faces of the guests were glossy and loose. I danced with various men, mostly from the summer theater, and one of them asked, "How do you get so happy? You're simply daubed with happiness!" These actors are like sticks of candy. You enjoy them awhile, then suddenly crunch them all to pieces — it's their nice colored sweaters, neckties, belts, pretty teeth, that suggest it.

Johnny Otto, an old friend of everybody's, a poet, was among them, vastly out of place. He sat with a piece of paper and a pencil on his knee, running both hands through his hair, and with a careful expression of cosmic passion on his face. Nobody listened, but he was relishing his newest troubles. "And that one," he proclaimed. "I'm worried about her, too. She's having an affair with a man in the company, I'm certain. But oh, what the hell? Let her have a good time, the sweet little fool. I tell her every wise, quaint, little banality she utters are the words of Jesus to me." His face glowed, and the steely hairs flew up from his high red forehead. He kept carrying the sonnet he was writing into the bathroom with him, stuffed into his pocket like a piece of cloth, and looked back suspiciously, growling that no one should see it. Suddenly he asked anxiously, "You *do* want to see it, don't you?"

A friend of William, the man on the beach — a sharper man than he — pushed me into an armchair in the library and knelt before me. There was no one else in the room but Rake, who was trying to play a guitar in the corner.

"I don't understand why you are here, living on the beach in an old ruin, and dressed in simple red cotton."

"Calico" I amended stupidly.

He touched one of my legs with a tentative finger. "New York needs you. You must find someone who can spend fifteen or twenty thousand dollars a year on you."

I was shocked into laughter. Philip and I would probably be down to fifteen or twenty cents when we reached the city.

"Well," I parried, "if I have any value, it comes out of my relation to the dunes. I've tried to think my way into them." In my distinctly alcoholic condition, I was confusing the remembered little blossoms of poverty grass with the flowers he was stroking on my skirt.

"You won't be beautiful much longer," he went on. "You're intelligent enough to know that, and, I should have thought, intelligent enough to make the most of what you are."

"Oh, not in that *blatant* way. I should call that making the least of what I am," I said, brushing his hands away and glancing over at Rake. Mercy! I thought; it's impossible to hold to a design when strangers whack at it like this. We'd better get out of here.

Rake also rose, and we rushed to the hostess. Going down the path we found the early morning like a snail moistly astir, and we wondered where we could sleep. The motorcycle, leaning into the hedge, looked broken. Beside it we stood swaying, our arms tightly clasped together.

"There is a man in a little house on the back street, a landscape gardener he is, who would give us a bed. His wife ran away, and he's all hopped up. If you just let him call you *Annie* he won't mind your sleeping there. He calls me *Annie*, too, when he's that way."

"No," I said, thinking of Philip. "Can't we just sit around until we sober up?" And I thought in rotation, drunkenly: trouble enough — no more trouble — trouble enough . . .

Down the street was Amanda's car, in the front of her Blackwall house. We climbed into the back seat, but when we found that between mosquitos or enclosed gassy heat we would suffer in any case, we gave it up.

"Let's go back to the party," suggested Rake in tired desperation. We fell over a cushion on the wet grass. The house had emptied itself and was no more than a box.

"We'd better take this back," I decided. Rake yawned. "Maybe the door is locked," he said, "but we can shove it through a window or something. Or keep it."

"And ruin the ensemble of the sofa," I chided. "Have you no property sense?"

"None. I don't understand property."

"If someone stole your motorcycle?"

"Well, he could have it. The thing is, really, don't you think, not to care?"

"How can you be so disorderly?"

We touched the silent door of the house, and when we found that it was unlocked, we went in and left the cushion in its place. But when we groped through the darkness to the door again, we could not go out immediately, for once again we reached each other, our separate lives swung together, and our pulses were one beat.

There began to be motion on the floor above, and we fumbled at the latch until we were released. Watching from the deep shadows in the lane we saw lights flashed on, doors opened, and heard voices calling in vague alarm.

"Shall we tell them something has been returned rather than taken away?" asked Rake, starting toward the house.

"No!" I whispered. "Let's go to sleep."

The man who had lost his wife was handsome and polite. He changed his own bed and gave it to us. When the lights were out and his footsteps eased away down the hall, Rake turned to me with a groan. "This is terrible — this is a terrible thing." I was wild with having him this way again.

Afterward, when he slept, I lay remembering that each time this has happened we have been alert with physical timidity. When I considered Philip I felt a mingling of mischief, isolation, and innocence. Then I slept.

Now it is not long after — it is only noon of the next day. I am writing in bed. Through a confection of pink sky and green woods I hurried to the dunes this morning, over the Whistle Trail. Crossing the long slow walls of sand, which were still cool under my bare feet, I felt full-blooded and guiltless. I might try to prove that I had good reasons for not feeling guilty, but it wouldn't be true. I didn't have any reasons. Love is not a rag or a stone, but something that is always either growing or dying.

I came across the slowly paddled track of a turtle, and later found him, too. He was wary and busy, hastening along in his fashion, but

I altered the course of his life by standing close above him, and he turned at a sharp right angle and made off anxiously.

By the shingle the sea broke in long glittering rolls. I took off all my clothes and swam deep into the still water beyond the surf. Then I ran in the slight warm wind until I felt clean and dry as a shell.

With forbearing knowledge weighing down his brows Philip gave me eggs and bread and beer, after I had tossed myself in a frenzy of weakness upon the bed. I slept — and woke to here confess.

July 17 — Riding the night, the two of us, defying the lights, cops, milk wagons of cities, caught up and carried on the beam of a searchlight, a streamline of laughter, possessors of a vast country moonlight, and with a quick excitement partaking of tree shapes in misty fields.

All the time we were putting forth our power to reach and secure that city beyond which there is no other, feeling, almost with our hands stretched out, for its dormant attraction under the skyline. Quickly feel, before you know, I kept thinking.

Lights splashed by the roadside. Behind us incompleted experiences, and before, in the city, a new perplexity, but like a dash between worded phrases was the escaping freed journey between.

The motorcycle roared and sloped its plunge with a deft line. It had the way of neither animal nor bird; it was simply a black, yellow, and nickel machine with a body of cylinders, loud and strong. It did not falter, bank, or wheel, but split the air with a forceful precision of speed. If we were to go head on into a stone wall, or into the terrible bulk of a truck, we would instantaneously resign ourselves to the fatalistic luck of The Road, loosening our breath and flinging our limbs into the fall. But each wild moment is safe, one by one, as it opens.

White houses stand duskily, seldom lit, and they are too static and content; they are losing something all the time, losing motion and joy, for their only ambition is to seem to be old. They are wistaria-bound, lilac-bound, trig where the sunshine has lain along the flower beds. Witchlike, I could not give them pause, though deep lay a curiosity . . . But their cost is infinite, being care and the days of life, and up the hills and across the horizon we raced, away from their eaves and gates.

The moon fell away, the roads became dark, and a new chill imbued the air, the last chill of the night. The city held a waiting, empty place for us among its myriad places. We were very tired, with pained, dirty eyes, and we strained toward that place to rest. Down corridors of streets in small cities we heard that breaking hollow china crash of horses' hoofs, but through the country hills between there was silence, save for the explosion and rush of the machine. The western star slipped away from the roadside, but we found it always somewhere in the sky, above the left or right bounds of the earth.

We had to be excited, and the city to which we traveled had to be excited about us. Sometimes we said, as we passed a village graveyard, "Well, kid, we might as well go in there and lie down now as well as later," and sometimes we shouted into the wind, "We are the hope of the world!"

Part Two

July 19 — We reached New York at four o'clock in the morning and went down Fifth Avenue in its waking sleep, where nothing was stirring but the cloudy steam from under the pavement, and the policemen standing two by two in corners. At Eleventh Street we found the door locked, so we swung our legs up over a balcony rail and went through a tall window that stood ajar. Rake groped for the light, and a scene of utmost decadence sprang out from the vermilion wall, no less than Philip's picture head laid against an aluminum-coated pillow.

"How tarnished!" I whispered, before I remembered that it was he. Nothing I said could make his loosened features tighten into waking. There was a smell of stale alcohol and lemons in the air. In the other room I could not find any bed for Rake, and the sofa was a silly purple-brocaded love seat, too short and deep for any use. He bent down and touched the plush carpet. "This is nice and soft — I'll sleep here." He wrapped a blanket around himself and lay like a bundle.

"Goodnight."

"Goodnight."

Today he is gone, I don't know where. Perhaps he is on his way back to Blackwall. We three had breakfast on a card table and examined the apartment with mingled distaste and mirth. It belongs to a man who, I am sure, quite fancies himself as a cosmopolite. The furniture is commonplace, the knickknacks have no slightest beauty. Yet he thought to make the well-mannered sort of place which a man returned from abroad in an Edith Wharton novel could have created. This may not be true; this is my impression.

Across the way is the green lawn of a great rusty church. Around and above it rise the light pink and gray walls of the lower Avenue. They are all tall, with many windows, by evening fabulous — they are city, city, city!

Within, the main room is half walled with books, and more often than not they are inscribed copies, with letters from the authors dropping from their pages when opened.

The bedroom is an emasculated attempt at exoticism, and it will be difficult to sleep there. The bed covers and hangings are of an aluminum stuff which gives off a sodden crackle when folded. Everything in wood is dull black, while the tall narrow walls are geranium red.

In the bathroom are a number of cockroaches. Through its gray frosted window fall in the voices of other people in the building. Philip says one of them is a bit of a singer.

So we shall live here! We pay no rent and are grateful for shelter. Our friends have dropped a curtain between us and our poverty for a while, but we can't forget it is there always, just on the other side. Obviously Philip cannot paint above this purple carpet and in the swathed light. But Waverley says he may paint in Patchin Place.

July 20 — Here again I am on a city street, as once in Chicago, London, Hamburg — all eyes for it, leaning to its sounds. It is so far from the sea of Blackwall that I do not even think of the difference. It is simply another place, and in its own way as vastly active and strange. I stand by the iron rail of the balcony, strangers pass below, and this is exciting. Last night Philip's brother was here, and we had a discussion regarding these people.

I said that anyone is worth writing about, which Philip denied with anger, because he wishes to keep his scorn intact.

"If I reached down off the balcony and grabbed in any two going along there," I told him vehemently, "and they by some process or other became supine to my investigation, I would — if I were a good artist — make something of them. Of course this is arrogant to say, for beyond what I might do with them, they already exist with the original value of life itself set on them, but for the purpose of this argument we'll let that pass for the instant. Or no — it's that very value which makes anyone, *anyone*, worth doing. And they're worth consideration as human beings, too."

I knew he would hate this; and yes, he bent his head from side to side, with eyes closed in his distress. I felt vicious about the word which was so precious to him, which I felt he mouthed inaccurately. "I wish to live naïvely, or not at all," was what he said.

"Naïve," I kept repeating, "is the way a baby lives. *You* are a knowing being, and sophisticated, whether you like it or not. The unconscious simplicity of the village idiot is not for you." And when I pulled out an encyclopedia to search out the origins of the words we were using, it was all out of bounds the way his fury grew.

"Old meanings — pfui! Cast-iron words!" he shouted. And, "*Good* meanings, *right* meanings, growing straight up from roots!" I shrilled back.

Waverley smiled. And I was sorry that I spoke confusedly, but I was wondering, How have we come to be angry with each other? Why do you seem to be beating about against me?

And then afterward, in bed, when all was over between us for the night, a question went wandering through my silent doubtful heart: Philip, where are you?

July 24 — Our days arrange themselves in a routine of work. We waken in mid-morning and go through the vivid light of the streets to Patchin Place. On the way we buy the food we did not have at Salt House — melons, eggs, and vegetables that Philip touches with critical fingertips.

As I pose, and the hot sunlight spreads across the floor toward where I sit on the couch between two windows, the yellow dress sticks to my skin like wet paper. The veins of our hands stand out in swollen streams.

Philip's ringtail monkey is here, and it is sick; it sits on its tail, which is like an old wet feather, and pulls itself forward by the forelegs. Its face is nervously inconsequential and ridiculously knowing. When we enter the room it comes hurrying to hug our ankles. They call it Jo-Jo, but I am false when I call it that, for I prefer to say "The Monkey." I can't make up my mind whether to like it or not — certainly it is a filthy little beast. Yet once, when this same room was chilled and dark with winter, I came here, where Philip had been before he went West, and where his pictures were hung on every wall. In his cage the monkey stirred and chirped along with the slight hissing of the gas heater, and I admired it very much because it was not sorry for itself, though alone.

I remember how pure was the emotion of that time. If Philip was not there, his brother looked like him, and every afternoon I was there waiting to see the resemblance again. I lay in the box armchair, reading choicely under an aluminum-lined lamp. Sometimes the monkey shifted his position, prying daintily into his clever little hands that seemed to be encased in black kid gloves. The sound of gas was as constant as rain.

"Who fed you, Jo-Jo? Who was your master, Jo-Jo?" I would ask. "Don't you remember him?"

The monkey would let his hands reach idly over the bar of the cage while he stared into the spurts of flame, like a man who rests his arms on the balcony rail observing the footlights at the theater.

July 25 — Toward night I return to Eleventh Street, and continue my own work. I get into a silk kimono and sit in a low chair at the back of the room. From there I directly face the houses across the street. Slowly the tension of the hot afternoon loosens; the light, which all day has been pale and rigid, is pouring down the walls in amber, while from under every window and cornice and fire-escape flow out the plum-colored shadows of twilight.

July 26 — Last night we walked over to the East Side. There were sliced watermelons under acetylene flares. In a store window were dummies in men's clothing, like no creatures alive, but flushed and smirking. The foreign people kept up a continuous amiable motion in the night; even heavy old women in chairs at the foot of stairways were always fanning themselves, rocking, and turning their heads. They seemed exaggerated in every way, and just then it was the heart and the best part of the city.

We walked hand in hand, but when we spoke it was with a certain sad hesitancy.

Again and again I annoy him. I don't know the reasons, and he does not say. Perhaps he feels that Rake spoiled me for him. It is with a dangerously conscious effort that we are holding fast to this love.

July 27 — We were going out to dinner, and I lingered by the table reading one more page. He said quietly, "How can it be that I dislike you as much as I love you?" We both pretended to be confident and amused, but on the stairs my arms felt numb and I pressed my fingers together, for they ached with the peculiar sharpness of bleeding. Up to that very moment I tried to think we were closing in, our lives integrating to one vitality, but evidently trying to think that is no longer of any use.

July 29 — But last night, at The Russian Bear, as I sat almost timorously beside him, he said that he is very happy. Then so am I! This happened at the end of the meal. We were sitting at a small table before a tall mirror between the windows, and we were subdued and our hearts beat heavily and slowly under the pressure of heat. The warm evening hung above the city like an overturned dusky voluptuous flower.

In the corner, under the balalaika musicians, was a group of schoolteachers from some summer school or other, who clapped their hands with such eager cracks, indeed almost in a frenzy, that the leader finally was obliged to bow and smile at them. Near us sat a Frenchwoman, smart and meager, who jerked to the music as she ate. The mustaches of her companion had just that day been removed, and the gray naked upper lip suggested that he was but recently from his grave and licensed to be up and out again. An electric fan spun the air with false and unrefreshing winds, and kept in faint silky motion one of the bizarre lampshades hanging down from the high ceiling. You will see, and I knew all the time, that the setting was correct for happiness.

For a while the lights were not turned on. His brother was not with us. I felt deeply in love with him. And afterward, too.

July 30 — Early today Philip packed a bag and went to City Island, where Waverley and a girl named Marjory were to meet him. They will cruise along the Sound until tomorrow night. Waverley asked me to go, but I thought I had better work. I hope he didn't mind, because I do understand how highly he values his boat.

July 31 — It is lonely without Philip. Last night I went to the movies at the Eighth Street Playhouse, which is fashioned like the inside of a camera. I spent fifty cents, and so today I am eating only boiled potatoes. I have just now crumbled some of them with salt, and by eating them quite daintily they are good. It is night; the church bells have stopped ringing, and at any moment I shall hear his step crackling on the balcony, and then he will step in across the windowsill.

August 1 — Yes, as I wrote of it he came in, with the impressiveness of an entrance in a mystery play.

"You know, I was fairly *weak* with missing you!"

"But you should have gone along. It was very good, I got drunk, and cut my foot; how, I don't know. It's swell on the water."

It was sultry and we dragged the mattress off the bed onto the floor of the drawing room. For another two or three hours we could hear people shaking out keys at their doors along the street. Their voices were gritty with irritation and fatigue. Once I went to the window, and I saw over my shoulder, in the other room, the coils of the naked bed springs shining in the half-light like rows of blackberries.

August 2 — Rake came in today, to get his jacket and goggles. He wore a clean shirt that was too small, and a furred aviation cap. He boasted that he had put in sixteen hours for his "true" stories. I was glad to see him and threw my arms about him, but he drew back like a small boy. Wild colt that you can call to the pasture bars, but he will race away before you can put out your hand to touch or hold him.

I could not help going out onto the balcony to watch him push the motorcycle away from the curbing, adjust his cap, and then noisily swing around the corner of Fifth Avenue. I knew Philip disliked this, and I should not have been out there in my kimono, but it was nearly dark, and I wanted to escape with Rake. Who should also go down the street but one of those garage and radio mechanics who are always at his heels! He was in a home-made car, the kind that with a pointed racy nose slinks quickly over the ground. So Rake, also, was not escaping!

August 3 — As I pose I think of nothing, but watch Philip's eyebrows, which express a rejection of what his hands are doing. I listen to the sucking sweetish whistle of the monkey. When I rest, I throw my head back on the windowsill and clearly hear the crashing hum of rivets in the new jail across Tenth Street. The concatenation of traffic and building sounds, of multiple voices, seems to be on the verge of swelling into an antiphonal chorus through the summer day.

We have been putting Jo-Jo out on the fire escape, as a doctor says he has rickets and needs much sunlight. At first he kept creeping back into the room, but when he finally understood that he must stay there, he squatted on the bars, peering down and buzzing.

At nightfall we walked toward the East River. The air is still warm and thick as soup. Among the gaunt and cluttered wholesale houses were only a few people. In the back seat of an open car a negro man was propped against a pillow of suffocating maroon satin, and on a truck a pallid boy leaned in humorous draped ease over a pile of upholstery fabrics. By the time we reached the river it was dark, and we sat on the piles for a long time, watching the tugboats creep quickly across the water like proud comic cats with lights hung on the tips of their ears and up and down their tails.

We turned by the looming gas tanks, and returned along an empty street where only nightmare cats and old newspapers were moving in the warm windy silence. Our eyes went up from the pavement at sight of a streetlamp thrusting its vivid theatric light into a man's pink face, asleep yet somehow staring. He lay on a fire escape before a brick wall, and he was wrapped to his throat in a white sheet.

August 4 — All the forenoon I went about leaving my name in studios. It is stupid work, posing, but we seem to have no money at all. I knew we hadn't a penny for lunch, but I went to meet Philip at Patchin Place nevertheless, and going through the gate ran into him with another man, a sort of theater director as well as a stage designer. He had a high forehead and a tired manner; I felt sure it was the prominent delineation of the skull which had attracted Philip to him. He took us both to lunch and called us "children," and we glanced at each other with glee because it seemed so provident.

In the afternoon I sat for Philip, but suddenly he said harshly, "You can go now. I won't keep you from your own work any longer. As for me, I wish to die."

He sat with his head pushed down onto his hands, and I stood near the door in sadness. No longer can I reach him, no longer is there clarity between us.

Now I am here in the apartment at Eleventh Street.

What will become of us? At one time he loved me "more than life," but now he says he wishes to die. I fear to touch him, lest I annoy him, and for the same reason consider every word before speaking.

Well, this is said to be love and couldn't be otherwise, I suppose. And I thought it would be peaceful! No, it is being in a panic all the time. If he should go away, I would still have this passion to endure, like the other things — like the house, like the street, like the oddly living, still living heart. Oh, now, my darling, will you come down the street? Leave your brother's place and come here to me? Shall I look from the balcony and find you are at least a street away, which will discourage me a great deal, or shall I not look, and thus increase the possibility of your step immediately upon the stair?

All is well; as usual I was an anguished fool. We proceed on the instant back to Waverley's, where we shall drink two bottles of red wine. Waverley is a businessman, he is rich, he is generous!

August 5 — The papers say we are having a heat wave, but being burnt out now, and dry, I do not find it intolerable. On Saturday, in the city summer, the pressure is gently lifted. There are scarcely any people, and by midsummer even those have a look of patience.

I have just been over to give the monkey his rations for the day. The two brothers have gone away, cruising again. This time Waverley's girl Marjory did not go, nor did they say anything about my going, either. I wonder if I have been rude? I should have gone when Waverley asked me last time — it was only that I craved the discipline of being alone.

August 6 — A poor day, but not *too* poor. Philip is just back from the cordial shop without alcohol. Waverley is here. I posed; it was very warm in the afternoon. When the day turned and cooled, we went to the Café Royal for dinner and sat outside on the pavement. As we watched the people entering and leaving, our faces blanched with the strain of curiosity. The place has provocative vitality. When the telephone rings, and the name of one of the Jewish actors is called, he marches among the tables with dark, almost glowering pride. The women are seldom beautiful, but they are animated in individual ways. The men look like journalists and talk emphatically. The thing is to order a cold *borscht*.

Where we get our money I scarcely know, but we always seem to have a little bit. Philip's family is wealthy, but they will not help him, because they built a house for their two boys, in Toledo, and now the boys won't live there. But once this summer they sent him twenty dollars, and once I made another twenty dollars from a story. It makes me laugh to be in a roomful of bijoux and plush, yet without any money.

One night a novelist and an army widow came to call. (There was a year when I didn't care what I was doing, and I used to whistle under his window in the middle of the night. I was always walking around in the middle of the night at that time, and I often slept on the beach near the village.) It was surprising to see them. We gave them alcohol with ginger ale and lemons, but without any ice, and soon after Philip slipped away.

"My brother is expecting me to help him bottle some ale." I touched him goodbye with my fingers. Then I went back and sat between my visitors, on the sheets of the mattress on the floor, and all around us the room was queer, as if it had nothing to do with us. It was very like drinking in a mausoleum, I crouching on the white slab, and all the furniture memorial. The novelist threw himself around in the armchair, was dogmatic, and told anecdotes with tireless vigor.

The woman suggested that we rent out the books, first editions and all, in a circulating library. I looked at her with admiration, the sleek unfriendly creature. What a nice mischievous idea; it made me think of Rake. I hugged myself and rocked back and forth.

Very late that night Philip climbed in over the railing. In the darkness a faint lifting of air along the floor. We lay naked and motionless.

"Such a rampant man!" Philip exclaimed.

"Can you imagine that I used to submit to such a one?"

"Well, I saw a look in his eyes, watching you sitting on the bed, a sort of full round look — full with reminiscence, and then narrowing with calculation."

"Why Philip! Not as innocent as I thought. Why, how worldly you are, after all!" And this teasing delighted me; it seemed so much more wholesome than his customary aloof murmurs of "As you will!" I like him to be close and jealous. If only that I may be escaping it!

August 7 — We went to The Russian Bear again, and this time the hostess told us we could only come in if we sat in the very back of the room.

"But why?" I babbled.

"You are not dressed."

"But we're clean," I began, when Philip took my hand firmly in his, wheeled, and led me down the steps. She must have been annoyed by us before, as we had on the same clothes as always: Philip a chartreuse flannel shirt, baggy corduroys, and sneakers, I a calico dress without stockings.

Next door was the Rational Lunch, where we got cold grass soup and blintzes, so it was not so bad after all.

Philip wouldn't talk about this disconcerting incident, but only said, "It often happens."

We started talking about poverty, which Philip knows by heart.

"It's only when it's ugly that I mind," he explained; "when, because I'm not in funds I am forced to remain with ugliness. In a place like Toledo, for example, where the lives about me are respectable little dung heaps arranged with precision in geometric patterns."

"Well, as for me, I only mind it when I feel helpless. I feel helpless tonight, because I *cannot* buy silk stockings. It would be silly and wrong to buy them, when we have so little to eat."

"Come, come. Eat up your blintzes!"

"That's right. Who cares?" And we both said together, both meaning it ardently, "We must care only for work."

At home Philip drank a great deal.

August 8 — To the Stadium for an all-Wagner program, and away again in displeasure. We have been here before, high up on the concrete block steps, silent, seeing the small red fires of cigarettes in the round of faces, and the stars in the electric blue twilight sky above. Last night we sat near the gates, and there were voices outside that would not ever be quiet.

We wanted to hear both warmth and bitterness — it seemed to us we expected that of music, and yes, for a while the music was strong as anger. I looked at Philip, who lay still, with his full lips angled with his interest. Although his head was in my lap, it was as if he weren't touching me at all. Are you far away? I was thinking. No, no, don't turn, don't smile at me. I'll go with you to the far place.

After the intermission the voices outside were shriller than ever, and the music seemed to go on and on without any lift — round masses of sound without edges. I rose and whispered to Philip that

I was going home, that anybody could have Wagner.

With my last dime I took the wrong bus, and it turned back at Forty-fifth Street, so I had to walk the rest of the way. Men were working on Fifth Avenue, night men with underground lights upcast on their clothes, throwing them into robust sculpturesque relief. I stopped for a long while to watch one of these red-lamp colonies settle down on the ground and make some unknown adjustments beneath the surface.

After I passed the fenced-off section, there always seemed to be somebody following me in a car, calling out a sinister invitation to ride. Once I stamped my foot in exasperation.

At Eighteenth Street a girl came toward me holding out a paper and asking for ten cents "To Help the Cause." I said, "Oh, I'm sorry. I have no money."

Her glance sharpened, and she asked, "You're a worker, aren't you?"

My answer was sheepish. "No. I'm not a worker." With one more suspicious look at my clothes she muttered, "Excuse me!" and went across the street.

Philip came in much later, having sauntered about the streets for hours.

This was another day in the city.

August 10 — There are days when one is not to look at the sky at all, for it is nondescript and hopeless as a beggar. The heat continues.

Whatever it is — it is bad, bad.

We worked a long time today in Patchin Place, until the sunlight at length relaxed. When Waverley returned, soon after five o'clock, we cooked dinner there. They, the two of them, were packing their bags for the boat. When I heard that Marjory was going, I wondered that they had not also asked me, for I am Philip's girl. I stood confused in the small sink room, washing the dishes. A few minutes later, wiping my hands on the towel, it came to me in a flash that Waverley had been injured by my refusal of his first invitation. I could make it all right by saying that I would like to go with them.

"May I go, too?"

I didn't really want to go at all.

"Yes, indeed; will you?"

A curiously unhappy lassitude fell upon us after dinner. The two young men sat on the floor and dandled their fingers at the monkey. Out of restlessness I talked plans for the winter, and they averted their eyes. When they spoke their words were indistinct, as if their mouths were full of cotton. Yet they seemed to understand each other, as if it were a language of their own.

Feargus's son's wife, who lives across the way, knocked at the door, and I let her in. She was an Italian with a childish sallow beauty about her, and she delivered herself right into our hands. They had no pity for her, would not rise from the floor, and hardly talked but continued with a kind of listless ardor to stroke the monkey. The day *would* not go, but seemed to clot upon the walls.

Finally Marise went away. I was sorry for the way they had treated her and leaned out over the fire escape to watch her cross the court. Just by her door she turned and looked up at the window, with tears going down her cheeks. I really heard her speak for she was so vehement about it.

"The nasty pretty boys!"

I came to Eleventh Street alone, and in the dark end of the twilight lay face down on the mattress. On the street, the people I had passed — when I looked at them I seemed to go right into them, and they into me. Tired of the streets.

To pour out my hate! To accuse him of speech without significance, of snobbery, neurosis, and of unkindness. I saw the scorn in his eyes, and it makes me lie here quivering.

The monkey — do they lavish themselves on it purposely to fret me? "Children are obscene, don't you think so?" he asked. How obscene is that monkey!

This affection of ours is like a flower whose stalk is broken, but the fibers are still connected. We did not break the stalk, but *someone else.*

Later — He stayed away for an hour or so with his brother, then at last he came and talked to me with a gentle bodyless voice.

"What is the trouble?"

"I think it's that there is not enough vitality here. Perhaps I should be bearing children."

"Yes, I thought it would come to that. Unfortunately, I am not in a position to sympathize."

"They have soft skin and are much prettier than monkeys."

August 15 — Sails on the water stood like graven stone. I sat alone before the mast, and the water fell and fell all day long; under the deluge I felt I could perhaps create a new soul. The first night we put into an inlet near South Norwalk. Water and shore were flattened out by a plain oppressive sky, and mist came down as thick and wet as rain during the night. Everyone was sulky.

Waverley and Marjory were the first to go to bed in the cabin. (Marjory is a mannequin, with a smart figure, amiable enough.) Philip and I lay on our backs on deck. The stars appeared above, and then by some ascensional movement of clouds they were gradually hidden away. If he should bring out his recent phrase, if he should speak of the sky as "nicely conceived" because it hung there low on its clouds, dim, cool, and vast — I spoke quickly, saying anything at all to forestall that phrase.

"I'm fed up with the sky."

His rejoinder came with a sudden concentration of impatience. "Unfortunately, I am not as sophisticated as you."

I faced him to turn my stinging grievance back upon him, but in the instant knew we were going down now to the end. Our weapons were drawn at last, in anger, and now it must be finished in pain.

But what *was* it we were fighting? Not each other, all these days when we have been living in the heat as in a prison, not each other, but something or someone between us. What a fool I was, that even at that moment I did not guess.

When we went to bed, we had to lie rigidly clamped together because of the narrowness of the berth.

The next morning was under a dull sun. He shot violent words at me for some pointless thing I said. I couldn't half tell why I spoke that way, except that I was nervous. It went like this:

"What is the ending of *Les Enfants terribles*?" asked Marjory. "I think maybe I've read it."

"We'll have to go up in the bow while I tell you. Philip hasn't read it yet, and we mustn't spoil it for him," I answered, smirking witlessly.

"Jesus Christ!" he ground out between his teeth. "Don't be childish. Tell her the goddamned ending, and stop making such a fuss about it."

I retreated under the sail and stretched out there until Waverley, looking through me to the horizon, said I was in the line of vision and he couldn't steer.

Marjory kept close beside me, and we whispered together.

"What's the matter?" she asked. "Waverley isn't paying any attention to me." When we glanced back over our shoulders, the two brothers were sitting stiffly beside the wheel in a blaze of silence.

"It's awful that we can't get off the boat," I said. "I'm getting claustrophobia on the open sea!" We began to choke with laughter, but I really felt ill with my inability to get no more than twenty-eight feet from an enemy, and hanging off the side I vomited emotionally into the water.

"Let's write a play," Marjory said, hugging her knees. "I'm terribly bored."

"Yes, all about how we dropped off the side of the boat and sank like dead weights. The brothers stared ahead and drove the boat past the bubbles we made. But we came across a submarine, and that night on the Bowery — Zut! the water through which we sink is soundless and transparent. The eyes of the sailors are like water. Our white limbs, sinking, are even less than negligible to Waverley and Philip, until meeting them on the Bowery they are reenchanted. We are now with the sailors, and we are wearing short black-and-white Apache skirts, but trifles of seaweed linger in our damp hair, and — " Thus we concocted some laughter.

Suddenly Marjory sobered. "I *loathe* boats. They needn't ever ask me again."

"How unreal it all is — our going on and on over the water without speaking to them," I responded. "But it wouldn't be so unreal if I could do something with the wheel or ropes, especially ropes. They're good real things to handle, almost alive with their own solid swiftness."

"If Waverley caught you tying knots, or touching his wheel, he'd go crazy!"

Late on Sunday afternoon, when we were going back toward City Island, I slipped to the stern of the yawl with the Cocteau under my arm. Waverley did not move aside as I passed, and I nearly lost my footing. Marjory saw this antic and winked dolefully. I lay flat, and when no one was looking I reached down and laid the book on the wake. It went floating back and quickly disappeared.

"It is the story of my life, which, unfolded, is passing away," I murmured to myself, more ruefully than accurately, as I watched its voyage. Certainly I got a great deal of satisfaction in answering one of Philip's tense savage questions, in the harbor that night, with a tight-lipped, "The book? I don't know where it is." And at a quizzical glance from Marjory I added, "I drowned it."

So now where was my nice, new, waterwashed soul? Walking down moist paths by unknown houses I kept shuddering. In New York, going down the dry irregular pavement of Eleventh Street, I said to Philip, "You treated me like a truckdriver's woman, and only over trivialities."

He lifted his head in the air. "We will speak of that when we are rested."

The next day had us in its vise even before we waked. While I posed, I kept thinking of the word *Courage,* hanging onto it almost with petulance. I thought I had better go back to Blackwall as soon as the picture is finished.

Now and then we talked of the yawl, and casually Philip revealed that Marjory had invited herself on the trip, that when I also proposed myself it was almost more than Waverley could bear. He and Philip had wished to be alone.

When their predicament flashed upon me at last, I flung about with dismay. "But I didn't want to go! If you had only given me the slightest hint." And still I didn't understand it all. There was something more that these words had not unsnared.

We were weak and tired, moving lightly, as if at any material touch we would crumble.

In the evening, when Waverley came home, I didn't want to see him and went across the court to visit Marise. She wasn't there. On the staircase, returning, I heard Waverley's voice. "You *know* I don't want her here all the time."

I went to Eleventh Street, and when Philip appeared I said, "I overheard Waverley talking."

We stood in the bathroom, where I was washing clothes.

"Yes. You see, Judith — we think, Waverley and I, that you are not quite sensitive." His voice was very low, and I hardly caught the words. Then I understood. Sensitivity! the quality they valued in excess. Perhaps in twenty directions they had been offended. Almost

I flung about with violent words. Instead, "How am I to know what to do?" I demanded roughly. "You are never clear. You say, 'As you will,' when I ask for advice. If I cook, you say, 'Why bother?' If I don't cook, you say, only half meaning it, I know, but still — you say, 'Lazy bitch.' I can't tell what is right, somehow."

"I am probably very difficult to live with," he excused.

I rushed into the drawing room and jumped down on the mattress, shivering away from the brink of these bad moments. "I will not tolerate the slow spoiling of our love," I told him with tears, as he sat beside me. "I'll go away quickly, rather than see it spoil in these small ways."

So it was Waverley I have been fighting; it is Waverley who wants him. It is not wanton jealousy of a mere boat that I have been feeling; it is jealousy of a brother, of another kind of love. We have been in a sort of swamp, the swamp of this summer, struggling in the steamy heat to escape a muddy sagging undertow, and I have not recognized the figure on the shore which beckons our collapsed hands apart. I know now.

I know more — that we have not kept ourselves apart in pride, as we planned to do, how confidently, but in mysterious distress. And we are alive with only the hardness of nouns, of these very words, for instance: pride, mystery, and distress! I remember that little longer than a month ago, at Salt House, I wanted the mobility of verbs about our lives. We have failed — that is the outstanding thing about us now, and failing is not a desirable verb, for it is done with, it does not move.

"The picture?" I asked. "After all, I can't desert that."

"Will you stay?" he said.

Suddenly I broke. "I'm sorry," I whimpered. "I hardly know for what — one crudity or another; intruding on Waverley I guess it is. I'm sorry."

In the breathless night we embraced stickily. Then he turned away, saying, "It's too warm for an emotional crisis, isn't it?"

"Yes," I answered soberly, but deep in me I sobbed with gaiety. "An emotional crisis" — what a phrase for the act for which there is no word! And my own strength grew in me again.

No hurt, conceived in me, shall pass beyond my private notion of it; no hurt shall be conceived save in silence.

August 16 — A thin blue smoke of heat pours through the city. I knew I would lose every trace of Rake as soon as he left here. But I have a letter from Martin: *I haven't been seeing much of Rake lately, both of us being more or less rapt (and I said rapt) up in personal affairs. His is blond. Once in a while I come out of a doze at some joint, usually The Spotlight, and find him grimacing madly across the counter, but I never can concentrate long enough to start a conversation. He does ride back and forth on his cycle pretty much, but did you ever try to catch a bullet?*

Luncheon at the Modern Opinion. The food was good, and I tried to get as much of it into me as possible while the editors were talking with an economist guest. (We have only a quarter left, which Philip, waking first this morning, left for me in the center of a sheet of paper, with his message written in a wide circle: *Judith — How insignificant it appears in the center of an expanse of white paper! It will probably provide you with carfare and cigarettes . . . however . . . Enjoy yourself . . . I go to work.*)

These editors were discussing certain scandals in the production of ergot, and when, at the end of the meal, they were through, the dramatic editor asked ingenuously, "Oh, by the way, what *is* ergot?' The others looked disturbed by this tardy interest. After luncheon, as I was saying goodbye and thank you, this same man pointed to a workman who stood below the window. "Curious!" he remarked. "He is like an El Greco."

It seemed so to him, I think, because the intense sunlight blackened the workman and he looked rather cut out of stone than real.

These days, unbroken by rain, are becoming by imperceptible degrees almost solid. And the nights, having no murkiness, are blank. I long for fluid weather again.

August 17 — Last night a theater man took us to dinner, this time a friend of mine, Van Danton. He has been both actor and director, and, like so many people of the stage, he is pleased with easy ideas. After he tells an anecdote he opens his mouth wide, and one is kept watching for his bared pointed teeth as cues to laughter. Just as your appreciation has subsided, he picks it up by fastening you with his quick eyes, and you have to respond again. He turns individuals into amenable audiences, but they will not remain swayed, and recover, harboring fundamental resentments.

We went to the Royal, where we ate in comfortable listlessness on the pavement, beneath two globes of light pure and opaque at the same time, like spots of fluid, brighter than milk, and enclosed by the hedge that surrounded us like a breaking wave. The shadows in the hedge, being driven down from above by artificial light, did not lie at the bases of the leaves as they do in the woods.

"I come here often to see the evening coming in," said Van. "When you are sitting outside in a corner, back against the wall, as we are now, the sky over Second Avenue is as wide and open as a river, and you can actually see the clouds driving over and changing color."

"I thought you the complete city man; I thought you wouldn't care to notice such things." I heard an undercurrent of venom in Philip's words.

Van bridled. "Oh, we city men have our perceptions. You'd be surprised," and he showed his teeth.

I sat thinking how the streetlights coming on drew a sudden line through the evening, so that it lost the long, slow, natural completion which it has in the country. And I remembered the long twilights when Rake and I lay on the bunk in the sea chamber — oh, memory, memory — why have I fled what I now want back again?

A cat prowled about our legs, and Van dropped him over the lattice. Two waiters engaged themselves in a quarrel concerning *zwei dollar.* Simultaneously, both wanting air, they flew to a window and flung it open, and in another concerted movement returned to their corner and their arguments. There were the same recurrent flurries about telephones as always. Next to us three dark women quickened to talk. "She lost about forty pounds." They fell back in amazement, they leaned forward with gestures.

We were here as in a vacuum, eating, watching, no longer talking. But once we smiled back and forth, when an expansive aged figure in full beard rose, placed an extraordinary square derby upon the top of his head, and went out the revolving doors with the festive propriety of a boat leaving a harbor.

Returning along Second Avenue we saw the doorman of a Rumanian nightclub sitting tipped against the wall to drink a huge cup of tea. Old women were pushing home their pretzel wagons. A negro eyed a red bathrobe with purple flowers, which swung in the middle of an arcade entrance above his head, and which was marked 50c. A window was pasted with a sign: "We Laugh at Competition." We saw a man who, although he had a strawberry mark spread across his face, was obliged to parade a sandwich board and wear, ludicrously, a lampshade on his head. All the life here is right on the surface.

Back on Eleventh Street we drank, isolating ourselves from the room as usual by sitting on the floor. After Van left, Philip began to have spasms of pain, and we prowled in a sort of nightmare from street to street.

Once I left him stretched on his back across a table of a lunchroom on Sixth Avenue, and ran, panting, to a drugstore in Sheridan Square, where once before, about two years ago, he had been given an opiate that drowned the pain. But a new clerk was there, who would not believe that I needed more than a pink bismuth, though I raised my hands in the air to implore him.

The men in the lunchroom said that we had better go to St. Agnes' Hospital, but as we had no money, we dared not. When I saw, however, that Philip was sweating, and griped over and over again, I decided we would have to go there anyway. Zigzagging from curbstone to doorways we moved. The last, most agonizing stop of all was across the road from the fantastic enameled turrets of a hamburg shop, and the white glare must have burned into Philip as pain itself.

Behind a screen an intern in pajamas and bathrobe examined him, could not understand the condition, and suggested that he stay the night. I left him.

This morning I rose early, and the day began to unroll itself, though without him I was unable to work. It is as if only the business of expecting him at each day's end, and then having him, has held this place together at all. I even dreamed, just before I awoke, of the furniture disintegrating into heaps of sticks and of the room slanting forward until it poured me out into the street.

When I telephoned the hospital they said he was comfortable, that I might see him at three o'clock. In frantic haste I washed and pressed my white-and-red voile dress, for I imagined that among the nuns he would find this refreshing. But when I reached his bedside in the emergency ward, he was quite beyond such trifles. They had drugged the pains, but in preparation for an analysis of the trouble they had fed him nothing but water, and he was beside himself with weakness. There was a crucifix on the wall above him.

At first he was quiet, only saying that he could understand how the contemplation of Jesus' sufferings could help these people in the free beds. We decided to demand his release, and sent a nurse to fetch the doctor, but he did not come. We waited for two hours. Once I got up from my chair beside the bed and read the chart, and again I got up to pin the torn tapes of Philip's gown at the back of his neck. The rest of the time we were both in a sort of lethargy.

All the activity in the room was at the dead level of pain. A negro patient behind a screen called, at first in whispers, timidly, out of his dark world, "Water, please!" but the nurse ignored the voice. Through a crack in the screen, I saw that a scarlet wool blanket had been drawn up to the man's throat, surely one last distress in the fiery afternoon. When he became loud and desperate the policeman in the corridor remarked to the girl at the desk, "Guy wantsa drink."

"His doctor didn't leave any orders about that," said the girl. "I can't give them anything without orders."

The voice sank into a continuous moan, then died away in exhaustion.

In another corner was an emaciated man with heavy gauze folded across his eyes. It was terrible that he did not even seem to be listening. He turned and turned.

Something swollen and discolored lay behind another screen, alternately swearing and whimpering. Philip said that the men had to pass him to get to the toilet. His nurse fanned and swabbed him continually, and the two of them kept up a sort of banter in the harsh and distorted companionship of his suffering. He must have fallen from the height which precisely does not kill.

My pity fell at the base of a blank wall.

Suddenly Philip pulled on a toweling bathrobe without sleeves or a belt, and in his bare feet tore up and down the ward. Faint with the mingling of hunger and excitement, his yellow hair standing off from his head in disorder, he looked like a woodcut fury. The nurse in the anteroom watched him with resignation, but when his exasperation was out of bounds and he started to swing wide a window and climb out, she jumped up and called the policeman, who plucked him back again.

"Calm down, buddy, calm down."

"It isn't fair to Waverley," Philip raged. "It's keeping my brother waiting." I remembered grimly that they were going out to the yawl again that evening. This gave me an idea. I took Philip's hand, which lay in mine without recognition, and said soothingly, "Wait here. I'll go fetch Waverley. *He'll* get you out."

Quickly I chased down the street, darted into Patchin Place and up three flights, then hesitating, knocked discreetly at the door. We talked without looking at each other, Waverley questioning carefully, and I breathlessly explaining. "Philip is frantic. The nurses, they seem to him to hold a net from which he can't get disentangled. He doesn't realize they will help him if he'll only be patient. You see, they want him to wait for a doctor and for a diagnosis, but he absolutely won't. You'll have to come — he's expecting you."

At last he was released. The nun who had firmly ignored my questions, who could subdue me as a woman, went down before a man. "Certainly," she said, in a hard reasonable voice, "he may go at any time. We do not compel anyone to stay here against his will. Marie, bring the patient's clothes."

The policeman tilted against the wall watched our distraught little procession with a fat smile.

"Food! Food!" Philip cried out deliriously, waving his arms in the open air. He took our elbows, and thus linked we sped away.

August 18 — Once in days will come a moment when the city is silent. Then I look through the window at the single emerald branch which lifts against a smoke-purpled wall, and as I look I am trying to draw in this rarity of silence on my breath.

Each early morning, vans roar along the street, and on the shaken floor I wake with almost a cry for the catastrophe that seems to be near.

I have worked hard for several hours, and now in the hot twilight I am resting for a few moments. I think of the early days of our relationship.

In those days I lived at the edge of a village. Each night, before finishing work I went to an armchair that was placed by a window, and sat alone in the gathering dark, looking down the icy hill. There was just a chance that there would be a letter from him, from Philip, in the evening mail. It only happened once in the whole year in that village. But I had not yet learned that it is better to expect nothing.

The streetlights would come on, and with their cold liquid circles swung onto the snow make the dark houseless hill unexpectedly strange.

I was always very tired at that time of the day, and as I put my head back into the hollow of the wing chair, I felt that my face was pale and thin. I distinctly recall that my fingers absently touched the hollows of my face as I thought of him. It rested me to keep whispering his name, over and over, in that particular time of day.

How good it was, really — the pure tired sadness, the streetlights shining on the cracked muddy snow, his name, and the chance of a letter in the box.

Then without inconsistence I swing back to the present, and I wonder where Rake is now. And it occurs to me that I have not fed the monkey in the absence of his masters, and must in the morning find the key to Patchin Place, and go there to halve an apple, fill a tin cup with milk, even speak to the beast.

August 19 — The telephone for the first time rang this morning. I was lying awake in the sunlight, my mind as idle as a half open door swinging in currents of air. It was Van Danton, who asked me out to breakfast. We went down to a French place on Sixth Avenue, but first I went to feed the monkey. I looked carefully at Philip's pictures on the wall, but longest at the watercolor of a barn and another of a woman's head, for they roused much pleasure. One day Philip said admiringly of Waverley, "He has an extraordinary color sense, don't you think?" The response, only now this morning, occurred to me. I would like to say, "The colors of his neckties and sweaters are taken out of your pictures, that's what!"

After breakfast Van went to Eleventh Street, and we talked and talked. He mixed some drinks out of the last of the alcohol. The Sunday daylight was banal and there seemed to be far too much of it. A persistent sticky music slid down from open windows across the way. After Van left, I dropped to the mattress and slept, for my mind was arid as a floor.

When I wakened, I seemed to know that in my sleep I had been crying out, "I want to go back to Salt House!" fretting over it like a child. Certainly there is no life here, any more. But I was sober again, and the air was cooler. For the first time in many days I felt no strain in my body against the heat. I haven't the right time, but perhaps it is ten o'clock in the evening, and Philip will soon be back. I'll hear the crack of his step on the balcony.

August 20 — I told him last night that my love for him still contains the elements of a beginning as well as of decline. Tonight we went over into the East Side, and we were serene and kissed each other at length in warehouse gateways.

This time we went along the prosperous section, where the smell of new bread sweetens the air, and the windows are full of either purple and red overstuffed chairs and sofas like plums, or long shining cables of sausage meat. Returning we walked past a sample coffin which stood out on the sidewalk.

Later Van came to take me to a party given by literary agent in the old Madison Square Hotel. This woman called me "Child." She kept going into the bedroom and coming back in a different dress. She wore eyeglasses, and her arms were brawny. All the other people were Russians or interested in psychical research, one old man having gone so far as to draw and paint by "automatic controls." He laid a great sheaf of these pictures out on the floor, and we turned them over. The agent drew Van and me aside, whispering in a way that was uncertain yet rather businesslike, "I think he *has* something there."

The pictures were imitations of Rossetti, flaming yet characterless beings in the clear colors of gems. Among them the man's hands looked dirty as old newspapers. He said he had given up being an artist when he was twenty-eight, but now these creatures of the ether had forced him back.

A little man with a pointed head sat forward on the edge of his chair, with folded hands thrust below his knees, and exclaimed only, "Yes-s-s! Yes-s-s!" to all that the old man said, although he was an important official in these matters.

A mannered Russian woman, expensively but not stylishly dressed, behaved like an actress and graciously presented us with her plump white hands to examine, by way of autobiography. As we were on the subject of hands, the agent beckoned for me also to turn up my palms, then tapped them and closed them with a smile. "Still very young, my dear," she said.

Afterwards, in Childs nearby, we had waffles and coffee. I said I didn't even want to laugh at their fakery, and Van said, "No. The old man smelled moldy as death. He smelled like poverty, too." I asked, "Did the agent try to hand you a teething ring, too?" and then we laughed, and I thanked him for the evening, for I do like to know people in New York.

In bed Philip and I talked until the milk wagons came down the street. I told him of the sibilant little man and the others. We were very friendly. Friendly!

I forgot to say that I have to go away in a few days; I can get some typing work elsewhere, and reporting. But that is not all — it is time to go while we are mended.

August 21 — Today was a fine day, for Philip finished his portrait, I finished my long story, and it rained.

I went uptown to the Museum, and coming down the Avenue at sunset, on top of a bus after the rain, the gold signs shone honestly soft and bright, and the taxicabs were like fruit slowly spilling along the gutters.

We went to the Dragon Inn and must have become quite drunk, for the two men, Philip and Waverley, carried me bodily down Sixth Avenue, one swinging my arms and the other my heels. After a policeman reproved us, they took turns carrying me on their backs. In the apartment they threw me across the room like a cushion and chased me in and out through the balcony windows. Once, as I fell panting, Waverley kissed me, and I screamed in surprise. Finally they twisted my heels over my head so far that I thought my neck was going to break, nor could I breathe. I decided that in reality they wanted to kill me and ran to the bedroom in horror.

August 22 — He came in toward nightfall and knelt down soberly with his arms about my knees. "I could not face the winter without you," he said.

"Then we shall arrange it."

I looked down, and I was very sorry for him, because he would have to be in poverty again, and there would be no fresh sweet novelty for him in this love of ours. It was an old thing now, with its intense familiar wariness, but it was inescapable. Into my mind suddenly flew Schubert's poem, *Die Krähe,* and though I did not like to remember it, I murmured, "Oh, Raven, for once let me see faithfulness until death . . ."[21]

August 24 — He has gone for a long cruise on the yawl, he and Waverley. We shall meet again in Blackwall.

Last night we couldn't sleep, and it all seemed different from what it had been. I felt like getting a tight hold on this relationship for once, and I said in a lightly musing way, "I really do think I love you more than anyone else," and then, because we don't commit ourselves this way anymore, I become shy about it, and added, "Or don't I?"

He turned abruptly from embracing me and jounced his back

against mine. I began to feel sad and ran my hands teasingly down his back. He turned around, for sometimes he can be kind. We reached for the light and opened a bottle of ale, sitting up in bed to drink it, and then in darkness slipped down under the covers. And he began to be very miserable.

The devil got in me, and I whispered, "Always!" It was then, for us both, as though somewhere something that had been high up had fallen down and been broken.

In the long darkness a faint light from the street found its way in and painted dim plaques on the wall across from the windows. Here the trees cast their thin shadows, and like tired fingers these wove gently back and forth all night. We kept hearing the strange distant thing falling and breaking, and when we finally went to sleep we were both regretting my having spoken this way.

This is my last whole day in New York. I stand at the window and I am bewildered by the surface of walls, by the tree that in the city seems also something built. The appearance of things, upon which I rely, here tries one utterly. It has to be understood, but in the country or by the sea there is no need to wrench at understanding — it is sufficient that the object is there, beneath the hand.

Perhaps in the winter in the city, with a variety of companions, one could develop a faculty that would resemble understanding. I can imagine that when the heat is gone out of the air, and the city is light and free again, we would absorb shop windows and find new restaurants, we would ride buses and ferries, and turn into the newsreel theaters — but it wouldn't be truly a sensuous connection.

August 25 — I hear the sweet rain. At least they can't keep the rain out of the city.

Philip and Waverley went away this morning for a long cruise, of some two weeks.

I tried to shake loose from some girls, mannequins or models they were, friends of Marjory, and they couldn't see that I meant to be alone, but sent a man, an awful man, after me. It was the final blight on this whole experience of New York.

His badinage over the telephone was disagreeable. "I've got a date. I have to pack. I'm going to bed early," I tried to say, but he only answered ruthlessly that he would be right over. I got into my most sophisticated dress, a green velvet, and high-heeled slippers. I had to keep ducking away from him, but he didn't like me well enough to be persistent. Soon after coming in he said with animosity, "You're no city woman, that's clear."

I wheedled him out of Eleventh Street and rushed before him up the stairs of a house in Washington Square. In the cab he had pinched me, so I ran with my hands protecting my backside. The people there were playing bridge in a high gray-walled room. It had blocks of black-and-white linoleum on the floor, and on the black glass tables were little animal figures in white bone, rows upon rows of them. It was a desolate place.

I took another cab back and fell into my armchair weeping with disgust, longing for Philip and Salt House, and didn't even wipe the tears off my face or close my mouth. Finally I controlled all this, but I am lying for a long time awake and letting the slow dripping of the rain from the gutters become, without blame, my own tears.

August 26 — Then a hot Sunday came, and I went to the Fall River boat.

And left that place. And in the warm evening remembered; on the wide bay remembered . . .

At first on the left shore were hills of coal, fire leaping out of low stacks, and sulphur smoke blowing with lush ease across the river. Farther along were whole street blocks of piled lumber, and then, after the last bridge, deserted, almost half the horizon around, was Riker's Island, with headlands of ash and refuse slowly smoking in the faint pinkish haze of evening. As it was Sunday, there weren't many boats: a few little tugboats swelling their muscles, a sugar freighter, and a four-masted schooner loaded with lumber and hung with washing.

On the foredeck beside me a boy about ten years old was trying to put the tissue paper lining back in his new cap. He was very embarrassed, for the wind tore it out of his hands, and it seemed to him that all the passengers were watching. When they were driven elsewhere by a stream of cinders, and he was left alone, he threw the paper into the water, but even then the wind cast it back, and wound it around his neck.

In my suitcase I had some slices of pumpernickel and several pears, and hiding behind a canvas-covered ventilator on the hurricane deck I ate these for dinner.

When the Connecticut shore was distant purple falling away into blue, I left off looking into the road of foam being laid out behind us and went into the salon. There, on the walls between the cabin doors, were plaques of dancing figures, artfully painted to resemble cameos.

"Mr. Dewey, Mr. Dewey!" called the leader of the orchestra, and a buxom smiling negro in a white apron and cap put his head up over the staircase rail.

"This number is dedicated to Mr. Dewey," announced the leader, and all the young men behind him grinned and nodded. They began to play, with insidious accents: "Little Girl, When You're Mine, All Mine."

The blond woman, who looked like a prostitute, talked with casual sureness to a man, holding her little girl's hat in her gloved hand over the balcony; behind them a baby in pink organdy skirts tramped joyously along the upper corridor; while below, the plain but nice woman in black continued to read, and one of the musicians rose and trumpeted with his voice through a megaphone, "Little girl, when you're mine, all mine . . ."

Part Three

September 8 — Blackwall. I found a card waiting for me in the mail here. "*Have left your mustang in coastguard's care. Use Salt House if you like. Regards to Philip.*" It was signed by the people who have left Salt House.

I walked into the woods, in my overalls and bare feet. I think autumn will come quickly this year, and it will be somber. There are some yellow leaves already, and brown edges on the others. And the wind sounds in the leaves not gently anymore, but there's a rise to it and almost a liquid edge. Behind me above the trees shone the harbor, lustrous and dented with light. The aster has come into its lavender being, hardy and small, beside the scarlet roseberries, and the seeded fluff of many plants is blowing about and clinging to twigs and slopes of ground. The hard green pellets of the goldenrod have begun to break open and expand with their yellow powdered flowers.

The gin tree held no bottle, so Feargus must have left the dunes.

Then I went out on the Hitch and saw in the sky the windloose clouds. On the sand the dusty miller has long since blossomed and is scorched at the upper tips, and its leaves have already faded, some to suede yellow and some of them to tawny lavender. The spurges, little delicate plants that lie flat on the sand whose thin coral stems trace out the rose windows of churches — they, too, have lost their green. The confidence of the crickets lessens, and they sing with faraway voices from under the driftwood planks.

It is a paling landscape now. I thought, seeing the grove of pitch pines from a distance, of finding Rake dead in his camp, and of how

I would secretly bury him in the sand.

This fantasy sent me back into Blackwall looking for him. Down the street in front of the cold-storage plant I saw two boys and knew by his height and his black hair that one of them was Rake. I instantly lost my breath, but crooked my thumbs into my belt in a careless way and by hanging on tight managed to speak without excitement.

"Hello. You've got a clean blue shirt!"

"Hello. We've been in jail."

"For Pete's sake! How long? What for?"

The other boy, whom I vaguely recognized as a townie, strutted across the street to talk with some fishermen in a doorway.

"Sit down," Rake invited, and we eased ourselves onto a top rail of the schoolhouse fence. "Snyder and I spent the night in jail for taking a car. We were really going to return it, and they were damned nice to believe that. We spent the night in jail and then we had to go to court this morning and be fined twenty-five dollars each. Amanda paid it for us."

"What did it feel like, being in jail?"

"I didn't like it. When the man locked the door I swore for a long time. I wouldn't like to have to be there more than one night."

I glanced sideways at him. Here we were sitting on a fence, with our hands in our pockets, knees jacked up, in the clear warm ordinary light of day, and he was serious as a boy who has been spanked and cried himself dry.

"If it hadn't been for Amanda they would have charged you with theft, I suppose."

"Yes. She was very swell about it." He paused, then added, "I have to pay her back, and pay for Snyder's share, too."

"Noblesse oblige?" I asked, with the beginning of a smile. He gave me a shove.

"Not at all! Matter of my having an allowance. Where you going now, Judith?"

"Anywhere: I was looking for you."

"Where's Philip?"

"He? Oh, somewhere sailing. I don't know — I don't like boats." I spread my hands to express the unconcern I couldn't speak, and even to express a preference. Impossible to explain that our separation was perhaps a delicate treatment and would bring about a recovery of affection.

"Come along with us, then," he suggested, and we climbed off the fence and with Snyder behind us sauntered toward Breakwater End.

"We foxed them, though!" Rake went on; and, wanting to talk about the night, Snyder pressed closer to us. "Yeah," he said. "Y'know what? After the trial at eleven o'clock we went back down into the cell an' ordered a big dinner. They told us the day before that we could eat anything we wanted, see? We got roast beef an' fried p'taters an' bananas an' coffee. The guy down there didn't know the difference. When we come down, he thought we was sent back to stay a while longer. He trotted out meek's a fool, and we had a swell feed. Leave it to Rake an' me! When Amanda come with the money and we walked out he was some sore."

We went around a house and knocked at a back door. Steps pounded down toward us from inside, and a Portuguese voice called, "Well? Who's there?"

"It's me," snarled Snyder with importance. "Come on, open the door!" The youth who looked out was decidedly handsome, in a hollow way, with black curls and bloodshot eyes, and later, after seeing more of him, he seemed to me like a drowned body stirring in some deep but listless current, and this even more so than Rake.

In the room we entered upstairs was a group of men, some of whom I had seen in The Spotlight with their stomachs close to the counter, their bare arms leaning on the stained aluminum top. All the time they lounged there they were waiting for some particular excitement which would give play to an exhibition of their supremely experienced boredom. They would glance into their warm distorted reflections in the copper heaters, and I used to think at such times they felt life in general to be thick and juicy, and full of a certain reeking manly savor.

Two of these men were playing chess. Neither one had any teeth, though they were only in bulky middle age, and one of them had a hairless yellow head. Rake named me to them, and to a man at the piano, then he and Snyder disappeared into another room.

"Do you sing or play any musical instruments?" asked the man at the piano, whose name was Perry.

"No. I'm sorry," I replied. He opened a book of sonatas and played eagerly and badly. Manuel, the one who had let us in, lay down on the sofa, and when Snyder came back with a tumbler of gin and water, held out his arms and pulled him down among the pillows.

Rake finally returned also, and handed me a drink. We straddled two wicker chairs and began to talk. The gin made my mind milky; I relaxed for the first time in weeks, felt at the same time mocking and affectionate, and found easily on my lips that phrase which always pleases Rake: "Not that it matters." When I said it, by a deliberate perversity my mind was suffused with the fullness and importance of things.

Perry played "Sweet Mystery of Life," and the two on the sofa drew their mouths apart to fumble for the words in a sort of raucous chant.

"So you were in jail, Kid?" asked the yellow man of Rake, unexpectedly. "How'd you like it?" There was a menacing bitterness in his voice. Perry got up from the piano, and the room was quiet.

"Well, sir, I didn't like it. It made me think about justice. I looked at that fat unhealthy old man up on the bench, and I couldn't see how he could possibly have the right to dispose of us — to lock us up or let us go."

"Have you been in jail, Mister — " I paused, not being sure of his name. This was not an impudent question; in this room it was natural to suppose each of us had been there.

"Just now my name is Williams," said the man with gentle courtesy. "I been in jail ten years. Just got out last week."

"Oh," I said blankly. "That makes you different from us, doesn't it?" Everyone in the room helped hold up the proud silence for an instant, and then, as if my homage had been sufficient, Williams and his companion turned back to the chess board. As it was Williams's turn to move, and he was a long time about it, the other turned to me. His face also was the color of clay, but of coarser, more pebbly texture.

"I'm in business for a *purpose*," he said, as if other men had other reasons. I felt that I must inquire, "What purpose?"

"To make money!" he said profoundly and belligerently.

It was the only time he spoke all the afternoon. I was relieved to hear scufflings and knockings at the door below, for there seemed nothing more to say to him, though he was staring into my eyes with persistent expectation. Manuel rushed down. Two young bucks, well dressed but without neckties, followed him back. One of them, in a black leather jacket, came in like a snake. He *wanted* to look like a snake. The other was flushed, sat with his knees far apart, and kept running his fingers through his hair.

"What's the matter?" Snyder asked. "You seem nervous, Rex."

"Me? Nothing nervous about me. Martelli's in town, that's all!"

"Whew!" Snyder whistled. "It's all up with you, boy. He'll get you sure."

"Him? Let him try! I got a gun."

From the couch sounded an immoderate yawn.

"Why is he after you?" I asked excitedly, looking at Rake to see if it was all right to be curious, and he in turn giving me an indulgent pinch on my arm.

It was Snyder who answered. "Good reason enough. He played tricks on Martelli. This is the guy told us where to find the stuff we're going to dig up tonight. He deserves to get hurt."

Williams moved himself around until he was in a position to look squarely at Snyder. Slowly one eyelid dropped, as if on a string. We all watched him. "Lay off him, Snyder. We expect to see *you* squealing on *us*, any day."

Manuel began to rumple Snyder's hair. They scuffled and fell off the couch onto the floor, then pulled the pillows down after them and lay feebly tumbling each other.

"It's swell to see you again, Judith," said Rake warmly. This was something I wanted, and I took it right in.

"Why don't you like boats?" he went on.

"Well, I'll tell you. They're all about what I most dislike — sport, endless fiddling, indolence or activity to a merely temporal end. And people on boats, no matter how nice elsewhere, they get — horrid!"

"Hm-m. I see. What a moralist you are at heart, Judith. Hm-m. I guess that last is the most telling point, though." He winked as if he knew all about it, and then we talked about Henry James.

Rake said, "Not that it matters, but I don't think Tennyson was so bad sometimes. All the bozos are crabby about him, but I think he's pretty swell sometimes. I locked myself up with some beer in Amanda's house one day and read him all day long. He sounded pretty smooth."

I nodded, "Oh sure, smooth!" but paid more attention to his next remark.

"Did you know," he was asking, "that Salt House is falling into the sea?"

"No. It can't do that! We'll drag it back!" I could not discuss the loss of Salt House, and I don't believe he really wanted to, either, for he changed the subject with, "Martin is married. He married one of the art students, and they've gone away to San Francisco to make a living."

Our mutual irony broke out at this picture of Martin with his spry mind and his fluttering gestures, of this Martin of ours seriously married. "*I like him!*" I said fervently. "I hope they'll be very happy." Then I added somewhat irrelevantly, "He'll be one of the ones to miss Salt House, too."

By this time the good midday gold, in which we met by the schoolhouse, was worn down, and the afternoon ending was brassy and tarnished. I had been drinking enough to want only to smile now, and not bother to talk to Rake, and I would not think of Salt

House yet. After nightfall the various men were able to slip away, and finally even Perry, the radio operator who was now a bootlegger, went away. Snyder stayed with us awhile.

Once the doorbell rang, and a postman delivered a carton of little blue books. Snyder opened the package and shuffled through the titles. They included abridged textbooks of all the important sciences. "Perry's improvin' himself since he went in the liquor business," Snyder said with respect. He began darting about with a broom, and with his blunt dirty hands arranged the music on top of the piano and straightened the shade on the lamp.

"You kids can stay here," he continued. "Nobody will be coming back until ten o'clock tomorrow morning." With delicacy he added, "Rake, you can have that room; and, Judith, I'll put some quilts on this bed in here for you. Just don't clutter nothing up! I'm doing the housekeeping and I like to have things right."

Forthwith he carried an armful of quilts into the room he had pointed out, and I followed, asking, "But doesn't Perry live here?"

"He don't like sleeping here. His wife left him."

I looked about the room, and there indeed were the lifeless remainders of a woman. She must have gone quite suddenly — hairpins, talcum powder, and a bottle of medicine on the bureau, and on the wall snapshots and a calendar with leaves untorn since June 14. A soiled apron and a kimono hung together on a black enameled hook on the door. She must have gone very hurriedly.

I followed Snyder down the stairs.

"Goodnight."

"Goodnight," and I bolted the door against — what? Martelli? —and contentedly climbed the stairs again. We had forgotten to eat, and my arms and knees were shaking.

"Goodnight," I called from my room down the hallway. What excuse could I find to go to Rake? I noticed a silent alarm clock, and this I clutched and started with it through the darkness. Just by the stairs I met him coming to me, and then all was well, and soon we were asleep together. I lingered awake only long enough to consider that I had done very well to find him the first night of my return, and this was mischievous private avarice. I find him changed, probably because of the other girl.

Light from a street lamp on the back street came through the window and painted the flowered wall, and far away were the sounds of an early autumn night: cars going smoothly and quickly along the road, voices calling, screen doors slamming, then the silence deeper and deeper, finally the real silence, and just on the edge of the end an old woman's shaking call to her cat, "Naughty boy, naughty boy!"

September 9 — I rose in the soonest hour of the morning and crossed the Salt House Hitch. I knew then it would be a poor day. The moisture of the night had only muddied the creaminess of the sand, and the early dim shadows hung from the crests of the hollows without interest or mystery. Yet everything that I saw rested my eyes with its familiar shaping. Suddenly everything was irradiated with a long-flung and splendid desert light. A breeze came running up like a thin tune played on glass bells. There was a pearly white plaque of daytime moon, tempered with its markings, slightly distorted, and balanced very high.

Even as I stopped to watch this incredible change it dulled and resolved itself into an ordinary day. By the time I reached the wooded belt near the house, the sky had become like pewter and the sea was loud.

A wind-blown rain began to spatter down and made little licking stains on my leather jacket.

At last I saw the sea, and it has gone under Salt House. It was rising up the broken bank and falling back with a frantic roar. The foundations of half the house protruded in mid-air above the cave of sand into which the waves had torn their way.

I gave it a dazed appraisal, and then taking off my shoes climbed up the roof. The sand has piled so high that I could easily reach it, but as I hoisted myself across the eaves a few shingles came loose in my grasp and one hand began to bleed.

In the tower room a young man was sleeping alone, upon whose winey lips I bit a greeting. It was Philip. His eyes widened, his mouth sprang open angrily. "Your damned horse," he said. "I found her here, and she has been nibbling the tender buds of my trees."

I didn't even linger to tell him — poof! he was dreaming — there were no trees. I went into the stable, and Jezebel tried to turn in the stall, and stamped her forefoot. I put my face against the hot fragrance of her flanks before I watered and brushed and saddled her. There were no longer any oats in the sacks, but numerous empty cartons of Corn Flakes and Puffed Wheat. Philip probably hadn't any money to buy more feed and had drawn on the supplies left in the house. I mounted her back, and when she had steadied between my knees, I turned her long head toward the town.

I went to another house, to waken another sleeper, and there I tethered her and left her to browse. "The bark we two knowing creatures now lip and taste," I told her, "is riper, and the fiber more pungent, and we shall feed here, both of us, longer than in *his* dream grove!"

When Rake, yawning, looked out the window, I know that my eyes were as glittering as Jezebel's eyes.

September 10 — But did he know I was putting myself in his hands? Not a bit of it.

"Where've you been? Where'd you get the rabbit?" he called.

"I've been out to Salt House. I found Philip out there, and in the barn not an oat for this poor creature here, but three empty cartons of Puffed Wheat! Both horse and man are starving."

"We'll take some food out there!"

"And we'll feed my horse."

I waited in the yard while Rake pulled on his clothes, then we went to The Spotlight for breakfast. In the feed store across the way I got a bag of oats and strapped this over Jezebel's nose. Before his eggs and coffee Rake indulged himself in a staggering yawn. After this breakfast he was still hungry, and we went up the street to Wong's, where he ate a shrimp salad.

From there I telephoned to Dangerfield, and the bootlegger there said yes, he would take Jezebel back. He was very agreeable about it for his children were fond of her last year. They called her Jessie.

I then started on the ride to Dangerfield, keeping the horse off the pavement and idly leaning down to clip off the weeds growing in the sandy furrows. I didn't like letting her go, but, as before, I have no money to feed her, and the only stable I have is certainly going into the sea.

On the way back, Snyder and Manuel picked me up in a raffish car. "Come on to Perry's," they urged, "and have a drink." Getting people to be with them as they yawned and drank seemed to be their only positive activity.

"No," I said, my lips shut tight.

"Not even if Rake is there?"

"No." I felt at loose ends, without anybody, without even Jezebel.

"Well," they argued, "you like excitement; come on with us tonight, when we hijack that stuff off Martelli."

"No."

"What's the matter? Scared?"

"No, but it isn't worth being brave about; I mean so far as I'm concerned. What's there in it for me? The bootlegger canceled my debts, and he's sending me a gallon of alcohol besides, in exchange for Jezebel. What more do I want?"

"Oh, it's just some fun — *you* know."

"Well, maybe." I knew very well I wouldn't go and asked them to put me out before a place in Breakwater End.

September 14 — There I took a room among others built into a sail loft above the water. The loft, with its overhanging balconies and outside stairways, tubs and boxes of flowers, its little green doors with set-in windowpanes, flagstone paths, and the picket fence, was altogether comic opera, and I expected the footlights to blaze immediately, with a welling of song and extravagant dancing.

It wasn't Salt House, but inside the door of my room I seemed to be miles away from the town.

Across the yard, in the fish sheds, I will see in four o'clock winter twilights, in lighted squares of windows, fishermen reaching into barrels and rapidly hooking bait into the long coiled lines. I will see little more than their hands and the yellow skirts of their oilskin aprons. I know, too, how it will be during the winter days, how, even when the whole coast lies stiff and awkward with the cold, the harbor water will still be alive and supple, and the shadows of the gulls will be like other birds falling soundlessly on the long platforms of the wharves, and they will be wheels and swords.

In the spring I will be going out over the Hitch again, and the fine bare bushes will be like smoke in the hollows, and the rims of the dunes will be blurred with the sand that comes clouding over them.

If I take pains to describe one more place, it is because I shall live here when Salt House is gone. I shall be losing Philip and Rake too. They don't have to tell me.

The day after I took the horse to Dangerfield I was sitting here in my white toweling bathrobe; I had put my feet into cerise velvet slippers with high gilded heels (Marjory gave them to me in New York), and I was sitting on a barrel before my typewriter. I saw Rake standing in the door.

"Insincere," he charged, pointing to my slippers. "Judith, I've decided your candor is a trick. You're sincere because you know it's charming." His eyes were very dark, and he needed a shave badly.

I handed him cigarettes.

"It's as good a word as sensitive," I muttered.

He lay across the bed and stayed about two hours. During that time we had nothing to say to each other — nothing! He could have done anything he liked, even so, but there wasn't any of the roused feeling between us that we were waiting for. Then he said, "Well, I think I'll go to Greece if I can get there. I have to go away, anyhow. They've taken my town license, and at the next offense they say they'll take my state license."

"You'll ride bandits' horses on the hills, then, I suppose. That will be very nice." Why was my lip twisting? I disliked this scene, it was dismal. I was working in a new room at the turn of the season and wanted to be free of that suspended excitement in which he kept me. Why did he linger, as if something here was uncertain, unfinished? Like a gift I had made to myself, I finally knew he didn't want me anymore, and I was determined to be content at knowing.

"I'll come tonight, maybe, if I can get away from Perry's."

"All right."

I trailed after him to the door, knowing he wouldn't get away, knowing I wouldn't see him again. I didn't watch him go, heard without flinching the noise of the motorcycle as it diminished, and turned back with a hard face, still giving myself the present of not caring.

September 15 — And what of Feargus in this singular new world of loss? Only at Salt House was his gallantry a real thing and his foxiness enjoyable. This morning I saw him tilted against the front of an antique shop. "How are you?" I cried out, sorrily enough, I fear, since it wasn't the old bantering tone.

"Poorly, poorly," was his answer. "I've had to see the doctor." Then waggishly he beckoned me closer. "Strangely enough, he put his finger on the spot. 'No more wine,' he advised, 'and especially no women!'" Then, "I've a new home," he continued, speaking not only to me, but also to the girl in the shop, who, black hair and a sprigged apron, is a little afraid of him. "One room of which is for rent, a large and pleasant room. You may tell any damn-Yankee tourist about it. It may be had for — " He gave an impossible figure.

"Feargus! So much? You'll never get it."

Now for this I would be made to feel guilty. How would he manage it?

"But that's the way you narrow-eyed New Englanders behave; you soak your tourists. So I shall not weaken and show a genuine hospitality, but prove that I am up to *your* standards." His underlip rose and clamped against the other lip, his eyes falsely twinkled, and the girl and I turned away convicted of his own misdemeanor.

Feargus, I have lost you, too. You are the same, but no longer can I tolerate you. In the last moment our handclasp was a simple fragment of what was once a friendship.

September 16 — But I have seen Rake again, after all. He was dirtier than ever before, and his shirt was torn in the back from neck to belt. When I saw him I was cut away sharply from the world of fear. That is what he does for one.

He came to my room. "Ride part way with me and bum your way back. I'm going to sell the motorcycle in New York and get to Greece somehow."

I climbed on the fender and hooked my thumbs inside his belt. We went by the Town Hall and by the filling station, and there wasn't time at all to see the Hitch starting away into the woods.

And through the towns, over roads smelling of tar under the sun, both of us singing, until at the Canal I shouted hard against the hot wind, 'Rake! Say goodbye! Here!"

There we stood in a ditch, our eyes upon each other, wanting to see everything at once and also impatient to be seeing details, and so unsatisfied. I looked at the arrowpoint of hair which grows at the top of his forehead. The smell of him was in my nostrils, the arrant smell of sleep it is, mingled with the smell of the roads. There we were, I smoothing my dress, he twisting the handles of the motorcycle and teasing me by darting the front wheel at my skirt. The thing was — we were wild to be near, but we had to be separating.

"Now go!"

"I'll wait until I see you get a ride."

In a short while a car stopped for me — two large women in front, and a thin womanish little man with whom I shared the back seat. From the window I saw Rake grinning.

Tonight my peacefulness is less defiant than it was. I can dwell studiously within the hollow space of my solitude, and I can look out from it carefully at the harbor, the town, the woods and dunes, and perhaps there shall develop a new relationship between myself and these places. In the summer I seemed to come into possession of them through the bodies of Philip and Rake, and now they must be brought into me some other way. I shall watch them.

The down-beating swing of the clock, falling coals of the fire, the tide rising against the wharf, cannot possibly hurt me.

This ending with Rake makes no particular pattern with the beginning — surely there's no need for that.

September 17 — Philip has moved into town, into the upper floor of a shed. Today he stopped for me, and we walked out to Salt House and broke open the stable. There we found Rake's last brew of beer and threw it into the sand, which soon sucked it under, and we washed all the bottles in the edge of the surf. Then we broke into the house through the tower, and in the storage room, now shuttered, built a fire.

"The last fire," mourned Philip softly. The log was burning in the shape of a pueblo settlement, with doorways blocked along it in irregular tiers. These fell in ruins, piece by piece. The fire's leaping and its steady glow, at once, made time negligible in the room, and the fall of each cinder seemed to have been preparing for centuries. We were as timeless as the afternoon in June when Ione came for him.

I think in these last moments I found the truth about Salt House. Perhaps when we were living here and our bare feet padded quietly across floors painted the blue of sea water, or we lay on the sun-hot boarding of the tower between the four windy horizons, looking straight into the deep sky — perhaps that unreality was less exquisite than stark, and it falsified what we really were. Would I have loved Philip Hatefield, or Rake Basque, anywhere but here? Would I have served as hostess, daughter, rival even (for I sensed his plots against me) to Feargus, elsewhere? The wide landscape and the bare walls focused on us; it was we alone who moved between them, and perhaps that is why our least emotions assumed a theatrical importance.

As night came on we started back to Blackwall, with the bottles clattering in sacks on our shoulders. We were talking very little, and often looked back over our shoulders with anger to where the tide was rattling on the bars. The wind quickened, and at the high point of the Hitch I threw myself against the sand for warmth. One star was distinct in the violet air. A gull flew down across from the sea toward the harbor, never a pinion bent, but straight, and true, and unhurried.

"We might live like that," Philip said.

As I lay on my back his face came closer, and at length his forehead rested on my arm. We were undergoing, it seemed, a wary, timorous convalescence.

We ate, in my place on the wharf, the old supper of free fish, tomatoes, 'gee bread and beer, and he stayed all night.

September 20 — There is admittedly something extraordinary about Blackwall, but it is in the early autumn that we feel — and they, the others who remain — the most curious mutations of sensibility.

In the harbor the water bears up a crystal surface over which sounds of boats, children, and dogs are peculiarly sharp, and the cries of gulls fall through the air like pellets of glass. The moon, no longer a smart accessory to dissipation, is cold and hung very high. There are no longer in the streets the faces they have known, but only a few plump tourists and at every corner dark groups of visor-capped fishermen, bolder in their taunts than before. They think, I suppose, those who remain, of the gay drunken affairs of the summer, and it is as though they are already old.

This last week, to heighten the sense of loss, fires sprang up where the dunes pour over into the woods at the back of the town, for an unknown incendiary was viciously active, and for days the streets, through which the sirens of numerous towns were whistling, smelled of heated pitch from the trees, and the sun, already murky with Indian Summer, was further rouged over with orange smoke.

Now that I am living in the town, I watch them, these various ones who are going to live here all winter. They seldom meet, and when they do each seems to have a furtive nostalgic expression. The autumn rains will come, that always come, and this will have its seasonal effect and they will recover. And yet I know, by watching, that they are frail as the weather, and that despite their poverty and old clothes they are surely not natives, after all, that they do not quite belong here and are really exotics.

Yesterday Philip and I went out into the burning woods. I understood that the situation was dangerous, for a young boy who adores him was with us. I asked myself as we walked together, all three crowding along the narrow path, how Philip had come to tolerate this lively Jewish youngster. There was nothing remarkable about him but his spirited candor.

I remembered what Philip had told me: "He stopped me on the street and said he couldn't help but tell me that he had been miserable for days and nights. He only asked to stay near, and he picked the lock of the studio one day, while I was gone, swept it, washed the dishes and brought in food, new shoes, magazines, and flowers. I told him I have an aversion for the roughness of a bearded face."

I cast shy glances at the brown eyes and creamy skin of the boy, who now seemed as pleased to hold my hand as Philip's.

For some time we had been approaching a warlike skyline, where above the shadowed borders of the dunes were great dusky flares. On seeing these, Sammy called out, "Oh! Let's get close. I want to see it burn! Wouldn't that be a swell drop? Wouldn't it?" His hand gestured as though he could mass and spread what he saw into a theatric arrangement.

"Excuse me!" — he looked apprehensively toward Philip, who only smiled with an enigmatic tolerance. "Excuse me; you know I can't help but get excited. I'm awfully young yet. Salad days, you know. But I don't mind being young. But even being young I nearly died. I was sick last summer — didn't I tell you? They picked out a red plush box with silver handles. Quite fancy. What a fever I had! Really, I — " He stumbled, and the interruption quieted him.

Sometimes, while we were still on the highroad, we came upon fire engines, from which rolls of canvas hose had been played out to the edges of the woods, and here men worked, tired and silent. But after plunging up a bank of sand we found ourselves quite alone and for a long time walked soberly over ridges where only scorched pines remained of all the green area, and the ground underfoot was of faintly warm ash.

The sky was covered with a thin aluminum wash of moonlight and was very cold, but in contrast, below there was everywhere a gentle woody heat. Like the campfires of strangers, flames sprang out in the hollows beneath where we walked, and now and then we plunged into burning stumps concealed beneath the charred moss and fine hot powder of the holocaust.

The boy, Sammy, became very gay, calling each new aspect of the scene, "Oh, pretty!" and continually looking about for more actively destructive fires. "Careful," warned Philip, "they'll take you for the firebug." Sammy giggled. Philip walked along quietly, lifting his head high with the withdrawn rapturous look which I now dislike and distrust.

Those blackened trees which were still standing, though lifeless, were like the antlers of great animals buried underground, and here and there in a smoking bush, as in a charcoal hand, was grasped a torch that glowed and dropped sparks when the wind blew against it. In fact, for days the wind has been a malicious force, acting like a mighty airy fan above the fires, which are thus encouraged to creep from tree to tree and hill to hill.

Still Philip did not speak, and for some time we proceeded in a silence which was only disturbed by the wind's continual overhead turbulance, and by slight cracklings nearby at the bases of trees about to fall. He took my hand as we parted an underbrush, and didn't release it. I thought this might prove to be a form of cruelty for Sammy, my rival, and so managed to disengage myself with a careless air, as I stumbled behind him.

After this incident Sammy became talkative again, and later all was altered when he dropped his foot into the burning crater of a buried stump and hopped about on one leg, with anguish that was partly simulated and partly real. Our laughter broke out afresh, mockery in the face of disaster which had not really harmed us.

"Come now, tell us. How did you like Edith?" asked Philip. I supposed that he was drawing Sammy out for my benefit.

"Oh, she's the girl I lived with," Sammy explained directly to me. "Too fat. Lots of emotions, you know, but not much real appeal. But she *was* a good provider. Oh, what a riot one night! I was piqued, so I went out and got into a rowboat and rowed. Up and down in the moonlight. She was piqued, too. Went to bed in *my* pajamas, and left all the cigarettes about, just partly smoked. Fretful stubs effect. I thought she couldn't really have smoked up all those — we didn't have that many. So I got suspicious and looked close, and sure enough, she'd cut them all up with the scissors and just lit the ends. So I'd see how nervous she was!"

Philip laughed maliciously. He was exposing Sammy's quick superficialities before me because the boy had pressed near me all the way. Defiantly I decided that this inconsequential sprightliness of Sammy was an actual talent. But the narrative of Edith could not be continued, for finding that the soles of our shoes were heated, and sparks were breaking about our ankles at every step, we excitedly forced a path down a hillside. Through brambles and thick brushes we went, onto a swampy level where for relief we drove our feet deep into wet black mud.

Sammy pranced about the meadow and chattered. If he cared that Philip called me "darling," if he was at all disturbed, he didn't express anything but excitement in the current distress. We had lost our way now, and seemed, in this oval of safety, to be surrounded with smoke. Finally, as we trod edges of the sinking ground, the smoke lifted in a certain section of the woodland and we gained a lumber road.

Viewing the wild fires, which were noisily breaking down the otherwise peaceful summer woods we had known, I saw Philip in a new light. He has his divinity, but an isolated and humorless soul, nevertheless.

Around a bend in the sandy road we came suddenly upon a

fresh outbreak of the fire. From a bank of leaves in the ditch was laid a bright yellow ribbon, and this was fast spreading among the low-hanging branches of chestnut trees. We could do nothing to stop its advance, for we had no shovels. Gilded in the brief brilliance of its destruction, the foliage hung, lighted from below and shadowed from above, like a mass of coins or like metal flowers.

In the sand of the path we sat and watched these leaves, which reddened and scorched in the light, until we were chilled and tired. Which of us does he care for, I wondered, or is he troubled to be centered upon so ardently? I knew that he was in some way disgusted and wished to be alone. I have learned not to care when this weary emotion comes upon him, but to take refuge within a certain difficult fastness of my own being.

When we reached the dark highroad and saw only a general ruddiness behind us where the beautiful untended flames had torn their way — the flames we had not fought but only watched — I entered easily into Sammy's still playful moods.

"You should see my bedroom at home," he said. "Of course, it's not like Blackwall in style, but in its place it's all right." His hands sketched rapidly. "Black floor, sort of chaste, and cream walls with red — red? hell, *vermilion* — trim. Lamp's a glass bottle, with an English hunting scene on the shade, and English hunting scenes on the wall, too. They're very masculine, don't you think so? Scotch plaids on the bed — they're awfully masculine, too."

"Oh, awfully." I could clearly see Sammy's short but lithe form flitting about the room with fastidious motions.

Abruptly he asked me, "Philip's awfully individual, isn't he? I suppose you know him better than I. He's rather hateful the way he is now, with his head in the air, but *oh,* he's so handsome!"

His tone was at once mocking and wistful. We both laughed, catching our breath, laughing at a feeble god. Then we clutched our arms together and went, bending and sagging to our own whistling music, across the bridge and again along the road. Philip followed us at a distance, his hands in his pockets, his long legs shuffling. Perhaps we were not struggling for him after all; perhaps, when he felt able and once more full of love, he would need us both. There on the road, singing and talking, the boy and I somehow tacitly understood each other, and agreed to this. And temporarily Philip was our common enemy.

"It takes talent to love him. I congratulate you!" I said.

Later, we left him and went on together through the deserted streets of the town. It was long after the middle of the night. At The Spotlight was a noisy group of firemen, Portuguese fishers, and town boys. In joining in with their conversation, with a rebirth of the bravado which is mine alone, which no one else can understand, but which expresses my joy in life, in the actual forms of life, I found again my independence, out of which comes my best appreciation and love of Philip.

Sammy raised his coffee to his lips. "Philip puts a light in a window of the loft when I'm to come," he confided," but I expect for days there'll not only be no light, but even the shades drawn down. I'll either go there carrying orchids or stay away entirely!"

He laughed into my eyes and touched my hands beneath the counter.

"It doesn't matter," I returned. "Come to my place, and we'll talk about him."

September 21 — We, the exotics, go into Snug Harbor at night because it is the only place with tables that is open, and we can be warm there. We admit to one another the fascination of Blackwall, but only to ourselves confess that we are, at the beginning of the season, already tired of each other's faces.

Snyder came in once, in a red-and-brown flannel jacket and no hat. He sat with me on account of Rake. They asked him what he is going to do this winter, and he said, "Dope, on the Mexican border." He is one of the townies they have influenced, and he can't explain how, if he goes away at all, it has to be something as wild and sinister as this place.

"It's like 'South Wind,' a little, the damned town," says Maurine, leaning over her coffee.[22] I know what she's thinking, because she came to my place one afternoon and told me. She's thinking, "Oh, go away, you fool!" and she means herself. "Go to Paris, that's the next stop after Blackwall. You didn't really think it would last forever, did you?" She is having an aspirin in her coffee to pick her up.

Philip puts his conspicuous head in at the door looking about for Sammy, possibly for me. There are glances and smirks, for much of their inept malice is for him.

Sometimes Carlton, who owns Snug Harbor and plays chess there all night long, raises his arm in the air and cries out, half-apologetically, "Whoopee, whoopee!" He does this because he wants the place to be a success, but the people at the tables look blank.

I enter and have coffee, and I am thinking, "Only the breaking bell off the Point, I heard. A black harbor and lights hung at the mastheads, the squid were leaping softly in the water, and when I listened to the bell I thought I would die if I ever have to go away from here." Little short words like these.

It excites me so that I have to stay up all night, until I am scorched and dry and tired with my love. Some young man or other comes in, shares his late supper with me, and we talk slowly, carefully, until just before dawn. Then, going home, I hear the sudden voices of the fishermen, and hear them rattling the oarlocks of their dories, getting ready to go out to the traps.

September 23 — With Philip I went over the dunes to Salt House last night.

But first I'll explain that the week has tired me, for I have begun to pose for a slight living, and between times I have dashed about asking questions — looking for news and feature stories. I have been running early to the wharves, at noon to the court sessions, and at night to the hotels. I feel as if Blackwall is a sponge which, freshly wet every day, I must squeeze. Because it is a new thing to make all these efforts at wrenching money, bit by bit, from these various begrudging sources, my bones were heavy as timber inside me, my blood without salt, and my arms would not lift. So last night when I met Philip and Sammy on the street, I suddenly sagged against the windowpane of the drugstore.

"Philip, will you go out to Salt House with me tonight? I'm so tired, and I long to see the open water." The damned simple words, even they tired me, too.

We crossed the Hitch, carrying bread and butter with the desolate Sammy left behind. The night was sharp as knives, and we strode through it like new people going to a new place.

A ground mist had filled in the hollows, and descending into its white vastness almost we thought it was the sea itself that had slipped in thus far.

In the shed there was only one blanket, and we slept tightly face to face. Several times we indulged in "emotional crises," admitting with amusement that it was really the cold which had wakened us to them.

Sand has risen above the sills of the windows of Salt House, but Philip broke through into the pantry, crawling headfirst across the table and down to the floor inside. He made coffee there and found sugar for it. Then, in the eight o'clock morning, we crouched by the sunniest wall and ate and smiled, exhausted, gradually warming.

Going into town, the daylight was a drink gone stale in the glass. The tourists passed in their big cars, born into Sunday from the dull wombs of their daily lives — clean, properly clothed, eyeglassed.

Tonight Philip came to say goodbye. It is the dregs of the day's cup that he, too, is going away. His family unexpectedly appeared this afternoon, in a great black touring car like an undertaker's, and as he has no money they have persuaded him to go home to Toledo with them, where at least he will eat, as well as paint, and where they will give him the operation he requires for the trouble which sometimes gives him pain. And he is going, I know, because he, too, has found some deficiency in me.

When he told me, he mockingly dashed his head against the wall, and we kissed each other soberly for a long time.

After he went, I leaned over the railing of the balcony and looked out over the harbor, remembering a dream I had last night at Salt House. In this dream he looked over my shoulder at a portfolio of loose papers which I was examining. When I came upon a watercolor of his, I found that its edges were worn and soiled. He said very quietly, and rather in surprise, "You must have it framed immediately."

Then I came inside to write it down that he, too, has gone. The night is cold, a thick frosty dew is falling, and despite the stars it is still dark. I can smell the winter in this darkness, and I am thirsty for the cold.

Their absence will press heavily against whatever happens. Just now there is nothing I can see to want, without them! Except to stay here, and to work.

I see that I did not come through them triumphantly, but with trouble. *Weh!* Hear the wind. As it blows with its wild prophetic sound the studio becomes merely a cold barn, and I seem to hear the surf from the back shore.

One thing becomes clear to me as I sit here brooding. I have outlived the unformed tenderness of those first days in June. Surely I am cooler, different now, and stern — or, rather, older!

October 1 — Everything that day — it was only a week ago — everything went into a promise of some sort of fulfillment, yet up to the moment when I stood, in the incoming cold fog of an early sea twilight, at the door of this woman, nothing had happened at all.

She is one of the exotics, so I thought I would make friends with her for the winter's sake. I was going to her obliquely from Philip and Rake, slanting off from them to her. She, Rachel Evans, is a fat woman with dyed hair. She is, nevertheless, fascinating in her humors, has a sort of abandoned dignity, and is surrounded with affectionate, though rather delicate, young men. Gross, partly humorous, generous.

I would try out my winter here.

She fumbled on the other side of the door, and when she opened it, I saw that her hands were all wet with the juicy slime of clams. She was kindly enough, in her slow panting speech, telling me the complicated reasons for the supper she was giving for several guests. The room, slutish and unkempt, by a thoughtfully spaced arrangement had the colors of a Madras textile. In its own way it has the strange paradoxical quality of Salt House, the quality — which I've described often in this journal — of appearing at once abandoned and vivid. Indeed, I am so obsessed by it that perhaps I possess it in my person! How amusing — to take over points of character from a house!

"At least you'll stay for a drink," Rachel urged. I couldn't tell her, of course, how much I needed a welcome.

Straddling a bench, I began to relax in the domestic easiness of our talk. Rachel was rolling out yards of dish toweling for a tablecloth. Suddenly a blue-sweatered boy came in through the glass doors and glided over to her with a stupid and unseemly remark as he handed her a cocktail. Rachel turned her eyes toward where I sat and told him to fetch me a drink, too. Now everything was spoiling.

Then a Russian girl came in, with her black ropy hair, heavy breasts that sag like tears, and her somber voice, a girl I like, not because she prefers her sorrow to all else and when she drinks it is only that her weeping may be loosed, but because she is strong in holding to this one thing, this sorrow.

Several men came in soon after, and as they paid attention to me I felt a little better. I wanted to ask one of the painters when he would start wearing again the fawn waistcoat with pearl buttons which, last year, had been his only distinguishing feature, but held my impertinence.

Another, a sculptor, a smiling little man with a long thin mustache, I felt to be a young rat, in that he was yet unaware of his own chicanery and dirtiness.

Feargus, too, was among them, and we nodded sadly. *If you can't choose between them* — I could see it in his eyes, almost on his mouth — *you will finally lose them both.*

And Johnny Otto came in, with his arms lustily around Ione and Loyal. We all talked at random, and I rose to go. Two or three women entered while I was pulling on my sweater, and gave me only the tips of their voices and looked quickly away from the edges of their eyes. Rachel acknowledged my not being asked to stay by calling out from where she hovered over the stove, "Don't be discouraged. Come again!" That made it all right between us. These others, her guests, had never liked me any more than I liked them, and it was mostly their party, so there could be no question of an invitation.

The door closed upon their accumulating din, and I walked away. The streetlights put down tents into the mist.

I saw how the winter would go.

I decided I would walk out to Salt House, which the sea was about to enter and tear apart. And as I went through the heavy sand in the shrouded woods, I thought how instead of feeling rejected I felt powerful and content, and though the day lay behind me, unfulfilled and lonely, yet somehow it had been like music.

— The End —

Notes

1. In the 1800s, there were salt works across the harbor from Provincetown, on Long Point, and at various locations near the town. Hawthorne here places them on the back shore, behind Provincetown, as part of her novel's lightly fictionalized setting. Salt works processed sea water to yield salt, airing and then boiling the water to evaporate liquid until salt crystals formed. For more on this process and on Cape Cod salt works, see "The Rise and Fall of Cape Cod Salt," New England Historical Society, https://newenglandhistoricalsociety.com/the-rise-and-fall-of-cape-cod-salt/.

2. In John Bunyan's *The Pilgrim's Progress* (1678), the pilgrim — an everyman spiritual seeker — receives needed guidance at the House of the Interpreter, where he is shown pictures illustrating Christian faith and values. Feargus may be inspired by the fact that the Pilgrims who arrived on the *Mayflower* in 1620 first landed at the tip of Cape Cod, before eventually settling in Plymouth.

3. See note 1. A salt works would typically include a boiling room, where sea water that had been reduced by sun-and-air evaporation to a kind of brine, or "bitter water," was then boiled until the liquid was gone, leaving salt crystals.

4. *Salt House* is set circa 1930, during Prohibition, when the 18th Amendment banned the production and sale of alcohol. The novels' characters make their own ale or drink illegally produced ("bootleg") alcohol. Prohibition ended in 1933.

5. Hawthorne twice refers to maids' rooms at Salt House, but this is the only mention of a maid. Some of the summer visitors who stayed on Provincetown's back shore would hire women from town to help with household tasks.

6. Feargus here suggests that god is merely a reflection of social hierarchy. This atheistic view chimes with his Communist leanings.

7. The Clay Pounds are an area of sand cliffs along Cape Cod's outer shore where a layer of blue clay is visible. The Clay Pounds are situated just north of the Highland Light in Truro, presumably the lighthouse Hawthorne refers to here. See "Beneath Highland Light a Singular Layer of Clay with a Mysterious Name," CAI — Local NPR for the Cape, Coast, and Islands, https://www.capeandislands.org/in-this-place/2017-10-10/beneath-highland-light-a-singular-layer-of-clay-with-a-mysterious-name.

8. The book mentioned here is likely Louis Grudin's *A Primer of Aesthetics: Logical Approaches to a Philosophy of Art* (New York: Covici, Friede, 1930).

9. The Cape Cod Canal separates the Cape from the mainland.

10. "Pointing" here means pointing with one's thumb while hitchhiking, the traditional signal that one is looking for a ride.

11. Socony and Colonial are names of filling (or gas) stations.

12. The quoted lines come from the version of Anton Chekhov's *Uncle Vanya* (1897) used in Jed Harris's 1930 Broadway production of the Russian play. Translator Rose Caylor expanded the original closing words of Sonya

("We shall rest") into a series of sentimental outbursts designed to appeal to American audiences. See Alistair Ian Blythe, "Love and Wheat/Wheat and Death," *Dialogue on the Threshold* (blog), December 19, 2014, https://dialognaporoge.blogspot.com/2014/12/love-and-wheat-wheat-and-death.html.

13. Monument Hill is where the Pilgrim Monument stands in Provincetown, a tower 252 feet high, dedicated in 1910. The Monument commemorates the landing of the *Mayflower* at the tip of Cape Cod in 1620, and the signing of the Mayflower Compact, before the Pilgrims left to settle in Plymouth.

14. Irving Babbitt (1864–1933) was a professor at Harvard and a chief proponent of "New Humanism," a conservative intellectual movement that focused on the moral and spiritual values found in literature.

15. Clive Bell (1881–1964) was an English art critic who developed the theory of "significant form," defining art by its ability to evoke "aesthetic emotion." A member of the Bloomsbury Group, he was married to Virginia Woolf's sister, Vanessa.

16. Wood End is the southwest end of Long Point (see note 15). A lighthouse there, built in 1872, emits a red light.

17. Long Point is a curving spit of land that forms Provincetown Harbor. Boats leaving the harbor have to round the point to reach the open ocean.

18. Race Point is the northernmost point of Cape Cod. Boats coming from the south or west have to round it, and then round Long Point, to enter Provincetown Harbor.

19. Margaret Anderson (1886–1973) was the founder and editor of the *Little Review*, an avant-garde literary magazine that ran from 1914 to 1929. Her autobiography, *My Thirty Years' War*, appeared in 1930. Maxim Gorky (1868–1936) was a famed Russian author and socialist.

20. Breakwater End is the West End of Provincetown, near the breakwater completed in 1914 by the US Army Corps of Engineers to preserve the harbor. See the Long Point Dike on the map on page ix.

21. Franz Schubert's *Die Krähe* (1827) sets to music a poem by Wilhelm Müller. Here Judith quotes the poem's final lines (*Krähe, lass mich endless sehn / Treube bis zum Grabe!*), recalled in English.

22. This is probably a reference to the traditional Irish air "South Wind," about the province of Connacht, "known for wine and play." For the lyrics, see David Bennett, "The Story of Southwind," Athens Dulcimers, https://athensdulcimerclub.wordpress.com/2018/08/24/the-story-of-southwind/.

Afterword

Called to Salt House

Allison Bass-Riccio

Amid the holiday season of 2020—with celebrations held outdoors or in garages if one was truly fortunate, on Zoom if one was lucky, and utterly alone for most Americans—I asked my husband, Doug, for one thing: a book about the history of Provincetown. On this three-mile spit of land, filled mostly with sand dunes, ponds, and forest, the town's narrow streets are crowded with five distinct and sometimes intersecting subcultures: Cape Cod natives, including descendants of the historic settlers of 1620; artists and writers; the LGBTQ+ community; environmentalists; and Portuguese families traditionally involved in fishing. Seasonal visitors mingle with year-rounders, who form the place's steady core. This landscape, these people—along with any transient vagabonds who take a liking to the crystal blue skies, crisp wind, and unique curve of the shoreline—create this little "bold town."[1]

That December, as people milled about the streets, I was just grateful to be outside, out of my classroom, and out of a mask for a few hours. Doug followed me into one of two local bookshops that existed then and asked the attendant, a local writer named Jeanette, for help. Neither Jeanette nor my husband could suspect my life would never be the same.

Jeanette showed him *The Salt House: A Summer on the Dunes of Cape Cod* by Cynthia Huntington, a book dedicated to Hazel Hawthorne. That January, as I read Huntington's memoir of three summers on the dunes of Provincetown, my heart memorized her lyrical language, describing bearberry plants, swallows' nests, and the path that leads to the dune shacks, where she stayed in Euphoria, a shack rented from Hazel. In three short paragraphs, she recounts part of Hazel's story, too: how, in 1920, during a hot New York summer, Hazel dreamed of a house on the sand and, with her husband in tow, walked from Portsmouth, Rhode Island, to the tip of Cape Cod to find it. Approaching Provincetown, they encountered a friend, Agnes O'Neill, wife of famous playwright Eugene O'Neill, in a serendipitous meeting. Huntington writes: "It so happened that Agnes and Eugene O'Neill were living in the old Peaked Hills Life Saving Station that summer, and Agnes directed [them] . . . 'Tell Mr. Mayo, who's the skipper there, that Gene and I said you were to have one of those little cottages.'"[2] Hazel eventually bought two of the cottages near the station, one for $50, which she named Thalassa, and the other for $75, which she named Euphoria. The rest is history.

Well, more like *forgotten* history. A quick Google search showed that Hawthorne's two published novels, *Salt House* (1934) and *Three Women* (1938), were out of print and nowhere to be found. I scoured eBay, online articles, libraries, and national archives, only to find mere snippets of information. Details were lacking or contradictory, yet I was increasingly intrigued: I had to find out more about Hazel Hawthorne. I was most attracted by what I began to discover was her unbridled willingness to be herself, to carve out her own life at a time when women really weren't encouraged to do so. One thing seemed certain: the way the dunes had called both Hazel and Huntington, "seemingly from nowhere"[3]—that exact same thing was happening to me now. I was being summoned in some way. More than anything, I needed to find Hazel's *Salt House*.

As 2021 progressed, my interest turned into an obsession. It wasn't long before I had devoured all the information I could find, from a podcast about Hazel by Finnish researcher Inka Leisma to a *Smithsonian* magazine article from the 1970s and a collection of papers in the Provincetown History Project at the public library. I began to see Hazel for the complex woman she must have been: lover of the dunes, lover of writing, lover of her children, lover of herself. I understood that her fierce determination, coupled with her long life of ninety-nine years (1901–2000), fueled a complicated story that encompassed a New England childhood marked by family tragedy, a brutally public and scandalous divorce, a bohemian lifestyle in New York and Provincetown, authoring short stories that appeared in the *New Yorker*, entering open relationships and remarrying, advocating for the environment on Cape Cod, and raising three children while two others lived with her former husband. I learned of her many summers and final years dwelling in the remote and rustic dune shack community on the Province Lands, first built by members of the US Life-Saving Service and later taken over by artists and others in the early 1900s. I was in awe of the visitors she had at her shack: writer and editor Edmund Wilson, poet and beloved chef Howard Mitcham, painter Franz Kline, and famed authors Norman Mailer and Jack Kerouac. After months of research, one can imagine my delight when I discovered that the path to hike to Hazel's shack was only a five-minute drive from my tiny Provincetown cottage.

In March 2021, I took my first hike on the dunes. Doug and I parked on the side of Highway 6 at Snail Road, where a dense growth of short, scrubby trees lines either side of a sandy path. A hawk hovered overhead and landed in one of the taller oaks as we entered. Soon the forested area gave way to sand alone; a large dune loomed above us, and each step we took sank deep as our breath became short and ragged. At the crest we stood perfectly still and surveyed the environment around us. It was as though the vast landscape of dunes had swallowed us whole. Time no longer existed. Civilization seemed to evaporate. Only the hum of a distant car reminded me there was a town and a world of people to return to.

In the far distance, we could see the ocean waves curling in the wind. We continued our hike along the ridge of the dune and then down the back side, past cranberry bogs—low-lying shrubs rooted in patches of water emitting a slight reddish hue. As we walked, I recalled Hazel's words, spoken before a Congressional Sub-Committee on Public Lands in 1960 as part of her conservation efforts: "Thousands of towns in our country are so alike that someone set down from the air, blindfolded, would not know his whereabouts, not one town from another. A person so set down in the back lands of Provincetown can at once exclaim, 'This must be Cape Cod.' He may go on, 'The smell of bay leaves, these curious small oaks, this ground cover—what is it? Like nothing I've ever had underfoot before. This quiet under the wind. These sandy hills. This dust-free air. This must be near the end of Cape, this must be Provincetown."[4] I knew instantly what she meant. It was a place unlike any I had ever seen.

As I reached the top of the second dune, I saw the first shack. Set back from the ocean, surrounded by a small section of low pines, it sat on stilts, hovering above the sand. It seemed so otherworldly, this place of shelter in a harsh, wind-torn environment. We continued hiking toward the shore and passed three more shacks along the way. I soon discovered that today there are nineteen dune shacks on the backshore of Provincetown and Truro, on land that, since 1961, has been part of the Cape Cod National Seashore. The first structures were built in the mid-1800s as life-saving stations (many shipwrecks occurred off the Outer Cape because of treacherous sandbars), and soon smaller accommodations for sailors, surfmen, and salvagers appeared nearby. Given the remote area's untamed nature and lack of human oversight, it became a haven for "free-thinking writers and artists who arrived during the late 19th century."[5] Writers and artists would continue to make a home on the dunes well into the twentieth century, creating a unique cultural phenomenon. In *The Shores of Bohemia: A Cape Cod Story*, John Taylor Williams describes how "The bohemians' diaspora from Greenwich Village began to arrive in Provincetown by the day boat from Boston or the night boat to Fall River from New York, which connected to the freight and passenger train that stopped on the hill above Provincetown Harbor. The roads were still mainly sand, and cars were rare. Apartments and old farmhouses at the Cape's end were cheap to rent, and on a beautiful summer day it didn't really matter that most had no electricity, indoor plumbing, or heat."[6] Suddenly the friends Hazel made—O'Neill, Wilson, Kerouac—made sense. So, too, did her zeal to live life on her own terms. But why did these writers go on to become household names and not Hazel? I longed to find her book, *Salt House,* to read her own words about the way she lived life in her early years on the backshore of Provincetown.

That summer I made reservations with Art's Dune Tours, a decades-old, family-owned Provincetown business, for Doug and me, with our neighbors Dan and Josie, to go on Art's signature dune trek. I asked if the guide could be sure to point out the shack that had belonged to Hazel Hawthorne—the one closer to town named Euphoria. The guide was excited to hear of someone interested in such a town legend and happy to oblige. On the appointed day, my body swayed as the vehicle's wide tires climbed the mountains of sand and our guide described the diversity of flora and fauna, noting with pride the dunes' ecological uniqueness. Then the jeep mounted a high ridge, and at the top we finally pulled over. I got out and inhaled the silence I had come to love so deeply on my hikes. My heart beat rapidly as the guide finally pointed out Euphoria in the distance, far across the peaks and valleys of dune.

With the irradiant sun, cyan blue sea, and miles of sand behind us, we stopped to pose for a picture with Euphoria in the background. I could make out the clothesline attached to the shack and the gray shingles on the outside. Quickly I calculated its direction from our stopping point, yearning to reach Hazel's shack on foot. I knew I would need to wait until October to hike anywhere close to it. From fall to spring, the dune shacks are boarded up to protect them from the harsh winters, but at other times it is customary to respect the privacy of any current dune dwellers—those lucky enough to win a lottery spot or an artist's residency through the Peaked Hill Trust or the Provincetown Community Compact (organizations that now manage several of the shacks), or to have a long-standing family connection to a shack. People stay on the dunes for the remoteness and don't want visitors imposing. In fact, historically, dune dwellers and other locals would yell out a hearty "Woo Hoo" when nearing any shack to alert the resident that their solitude was about to be impeded on.[7]

That afternoon, after the tour, Josie and I went into town to a local second-hand store in search of anything Hazel-related. I already knew what I would find: nothing. For half a year I had combed the internet for even one worn copy of *Salt House* or *Three Women*, with no luck. Yet, ever the intuitive huntress, I made my way to the shop's bookcase and its dark bottom shelf. Clasping the first book I came to, I brought it out into the light and read the title, *From the Peaked Hills,* and the first page: "In appreciation of Hazel Hawthorne Werner without whom so many of us would never have watched night become day in the dunes."[8] My hands trembled: It wasn't a book *by* Hazel, but it was a book *dedicated to* Hazel. Published by the Peaked Hill Trust, it was filled with work by artists and writers who had known Hazel and stayed in her shack, including the poets Mary Oliver and Harry Kemp, and writer and activist Josephine Del Deo. Most importantly, the book contained an interview with Hazel and one of her short stories, "On the Baltic." After months of searching for anything beyond the basic facts of her life, here were her words, her voice, in black and white. "Hazel is calling you!" Josie said, as I showed her my treasure.

That fall I had three clear goals: 1) find Euphoria on foot; 2) obtain *Salt House*; and 3) apply for a writer's residency on the dunes through the Peaked Hill Trust. The second weekend of October, Doug and I made our way back to the dunes, determined to reach Euphoria for real. Gulping for air as we hauled ourselves over dunes one and two, we arrived where the path curved by the contorted tree. Here I knew I would have to pay attention to my instincts. We trekked toward the last dune that led to the ocean. Drawing on memory from the summer's dune tour, I turned left before the final rise. The path curved to the left and right again, deep into a dune valley surrounded on both sides by *Rosa rugosa* bushes and greenery that clung low to the sand.

As we cleared the valley, there she was: Euphoria. Standing tall, her boxy frame jutted against the October sky. She stood majestically upon the top of the dune, like a watchtower for the peaceful scene below. She was by no means large, but her presence somehow loomed over the valley. The gray shingles reflected the Cape light, which ricocheted off the sand and the water, and then filtered into the thin and crisp air. I stood there admiring my discovery for some time. This was the very shack where Hazel had lived summer after summer, where she had written so much, where she had so generously shared her creative space with other prominent artists and writers. In her book *The Watch at Peaked Hill*, Del Deo writes that Hazel's "chief claim to fame appears to lie . . . with the unique circle of friends she courted."[9] These same friends would eventually return Hazel's favor by writing testimonies and letters in support of preserving the Province Lands and the shacks as historic sites, in hopes of protecting the shacks' use as places of solitude and creativity.[10]

Later that month, back in the throes of another school year at the international boarding school where I live and work, I received a package from the Provincetown Public Library. I knew what was inside: a copy of the first and, at that time, only edition of *Salt House*. The library had generously loaned the book to me for my research, along with Hazel's second novel, *Three Women*. I opened the package with care, relishing the first time I would be able to hold these books in my hands. The jacket of *Salt House* was tattered and the cover's corners worn. I carefully turned the fragile first pages and saw an inscription penned by Hazel. I found one in *Three Women,* too, the writing there unsteady, coming after Hazel's decline in health, but I could make out her determination and pride as she wrote, "Yours shakingly, Hazel Hawthorne."[11] The *Salt House* inscription was from her much earlier days: "Love, and I hope you'll like something about this, darling. Hazel." I felt like she had written it directly to me.

I soon discovered that the setting of *Salt House* is not Euphoria, which is the "Salt House" of Cynthia Huntington's book. Though Hazel wrote most of her first novel while staying in various dune shacks,[12] it takes place in a fictional salt works on the dunes, near a town called "Blackwall." Knowing the history of Provincetown's dune structures, one can tell that the Salt House Hazel writes about, with several rooms and an upper floor, is based on the Peaked Hill Bars Station, the life-saving station on Provincetown's backshore that, after being decommissioned, was sold to Eugene O'Neill.

Many textual connections to Provincetown are evident in the novel, too, including mentions of Monument Hill, Whistle Trail Path, the Beachcombers Association, Wood End, and Race Point. Descriptions of the bohemian lifestyle, dune dweller customs, racial and sexual diversity, theater people, and Perry the bootlegger can all also be pointed to as proof that Blackwall is actually Provincetown; the neighboring town, "Dangerfield," is Truro; and "Salt House" is the O'Neills' summer home—the one next to the cottages Agnes O'Neill directed Hazel to in the summer of 1920. Most convincing are Hazel's own words: "Oh, I did a lot of writing there. I published two books. One was about the dunes, *Salt House*. . . . I kept a journal out there all those years. . . . I'm sensitive about my *Salt House*, because much of it was about my life, and people in town were scandalized. [Laughs] The bookstore wouldn't sell the book."[13] I quickly devoured all of *Salt House* and then *Three Women*, absorbing everything about this brave woman who so loved the dunes.

Hazel wasn't overstating the prickly public reception of her first novel, which reflected the morality of the 1930s and even extended to disdain in some literary reviews. The female protagonist of *Salt House*, Judith, is an intellectual, a writer, a woman with her own ideas. Indeed, she has two lovers and is accepting when she understands, toward the end of the novel, that one of them is bisexual. She rides on the back of a motorcycle, drinks at a time when it is illegal to do so, and attends parties, staying out late in both Provincetown and New York City. She lives on the dunes with men she is not married to and discusses communism and sex with them. A *New York Times* review illustrates the contempt that met *Salt House* and Hazel in 1934, calling the novel a "little tale . . . too slight and vague . . . rolled together . . . none too successfully into a story." Perhaps most scandalous for Hazel's contemporaries was the book's ending, when Judith decides that she doesn't need either of her lovers to be happy and chooses to live an independent life instead. The *Times* review goes on to say, "The life the book depicts is . . . maddeningly irritating . . . and throughout the whole muddle one is sorry for her because she seems to be . . . pathetically trying to live down the standards of her associates and neighbors."[14] In *Salt House* Hazel wrote about defying societal norms; it seems she lived defying these norms as well; but these choices did not come without controversy, and even punishment.

Months turned to years, and I continued to feel called to research and write about Hazel and the dunes. I was all the more inspired by her, now that I knew her writing and her fierce independence. I became so connected to her that I named my kitten Hazel; she turned out to be true to her namesake, preferring solitude to the warmth of a human hand. Any time my research hit a lull, a dead end, something new and invigorating would happen, opening a pathway to the next layer of what I was to learn of Hazel. I was awarded a writer's residency by the Peaked Hill Trust and wrote by oil lamplight in Euphoria. I was asked to publish an article about the dunes and my time in the shack. I had the pleasure of meeting and interviewing many "townies," some who knew of Hazel and others who actually *knew* Hazel.

One night I came across an intriguing comment on a social media post, and this led to my meeting and befriending some of Hazel's family members. Sitting in a small coffee shop on the Cape, I was treated to stories of Hazel's proper tea parties, her visions of environmentalism, her complex reflections on her past. Eventually, I was given her archive as a means of continuing my research and writing, while literally preserving her legacy. The mass of letters, photos, and notes helped me understand *Salt House* on another level, the way it and Hazel call out to others, asking for this journal-like novel to not be forgotten.

Indeed, *Salt House* is written like a journal—like *Hazel's journals*. In a green composition book, Hazel writes the date, the weather, and in short, terse sentences the doings of the day, her dreams at night, her worries, her concerns. Her voice changes as she describes the dunes and the sea: long, flowing sentences that poignantly paint the imagery of a place she loves so much.[15] Like Hazel's journals, *Salt House* captures the time and place in which it lives. The dunes and dune dwellers, the rustic and seafaring life on Cape Cod, bohemian Greenwich Village, open and free love: these can only be so perfectly set circa 1930 between Provincetown and New York.

Until now, *Salt House* was a story mostly forgotten, misremembered, or undermined in its importance. Reflecting on the book's journey into obscurity, Del Deo notes that the town librarian "routinely buried it somewhere in the stacks, where it could hardly be discovered by casual browsing, so disapproving was she of the contents. I know of only one person who has seen a copy of this work; however, some reference is usually made to it whenever [Hazel's] name comes up for discussion."[16] Hazel's book, and indeed her life choices, were considered scandalous, a disapproval that reflected her status as a woman author at a time when publication by women was restricted, or what they published limited by the day's gender norms. As a result, Hazel and her book did not get the acclaim they deserve. Today the novel and Hazel seem to be calling out, "Now is the time for me to resurface." The new Provincetown Arts edition of *Salt House* seeks to answer that call: to give new and expanded reach to a novel that depicts a special time and place.